ANGEL'S REBEL

Wings Of Deceit

Book 2

SUSAN HARRIS

ISBN: **978-1-63422-549-6** (paperback)
ISBN: **978-1-63422-521-2** (e-book)
Cover Design by: Gem Promotions
Typography by: Gem Promotions
Proofing by: Ashley Brilinski

APPENDIX OF
CHARACTERS & NAMES

ANGELS:

<u>The Imperium of the Angels:</u>
    Rieka – RIY-KAH

<u>League of Dominious: Warrior Angels</u>
    Nathaniel – Na-Than-yal
    Abraxas – Ab-Brak-Sus
    Devika – Day-vee-ka
    Verena – Ver-ray-nah
    Cassiopeia – Cass-ee-O-pee-uh
    Adriel – Ad-ree-el
    Adair – Ay-Dare
    Saskia – Sahs-kee-ah
    Draegan –Dray-Gan
    Asterin – As-ter-in
    Makata – Maka-ta

<u>Seraphan: Disgraced Angels:</u>
    Ascian – As-ci-an
    Cadoc – Ca-doc

Takara – Ta-Ka-ra

Khione – Key-own-knee

Raisel – Ray-zel

Niran – Knee-ran

Non- warrior Angels:

Kalila – Kay-lee-la

Eliseo – El-ee-say-oh

Hannele – Han-ne-le

Aramis – A-Ruh-Mis

Other Angel's

Zadkiel - Zad-kiel

Akora - Ako-ra

HUMANS:

Rebels:

Raven Cassidy – Ray-Vin Kas-Uh-Dee

Hayes Kennedy – Haze Ken-id-e

Tiernan Byrne – Tear-Nan Burn

James - James

Niamh – Knee-of

Aoife – Eee-Fa

Donnacha – Done-ick-a

Róisín – Row-Sheen

"Hell hath no fury like a woman scorned."
— William Cosgrove

T he world is full of monsters with friendly faces and angels full of scars.

Two months had passed since the night Aramis attached me, and the depth of Nathaniel's betrayal had been revealed to me. He had fooled me not once, but twice with his words. First when he had used his words to convince me that helping him would be a step toward my freedom, a cunning play with words that was meant to trap me. The second time, it was in the elegant hand-writing in his journals that tricked me into believing he was honest and trustworthy.

"Well, now that all this is fucking over, I'll be on my way."

Rieka offered me a cold smile. "Oh, will you now?"

My heart sank. "That was the deal. I find your traitor and I walk out the front door to try and kill you another day."

I knew my words would only fan the flames of her way of torturing me and still I couldn't help myself as I glanced around at the remaining members of the League for help. I wanted them to have my back, but they all stood motionless. The only flicker of any emotion came from Adriel and the fists that were clenched by his side.

"You have done your job so strikingly well that I am loathe to lose you so soon."

No...no...no...this couldn't be happening...

And yet, I knew that I would not be walking out of the citadel today and to freedom. Rieka never planned on letting me leave, did she? Aramis was a test of my power, to see exactly what I could do and I had fallen for it.

"You heard Aramis himself; there are more traitors in my citadel. You will help me find them all."

My gaze flittered to Nathaniel who had the good graces to look downtrodden and defeated. I realised that's what he had been trying to tell me in the dungeon when Cassiopeia interrupted us.

"I trusted you." I snarled at him, feeling a sliver of glee when he jerked like I had struck him. "You promised me my freedom, Nathaniel. You promised me."

Nathaniel lifted his stormy eyes to mine before he responded to my words. "I offered you a chance at freedom. I never said it was inevitable."

I had not known that the pain of his savageness, the way in which the League had voiced their unhappiness, but no one save Adriel had openly told Nathaniel that if he could take me from this place, he would, could hurt me so much.

A low grumble sounded as I turned toward the desk by the window. Grainger, the stone gargoyle who had saved my life by alerting me to Aramis' presence. He flexed his wings and grunted, his black eyes looking at me until I went over and gave him a scratch on his head. Then the creature huffed out a contented sigh before proceeding to go back to sleep. His snores loud enough to wake the dead.

It would seem that my new roommate no longer felt the need to remain stealthy since I now knew about his existence as more than the statue that I had once believed him to be.

I guessed I was fucking oblivious and gullible to everything going on around me.

Since our epic fallout, I'd only seen Nathaniel once, when Adriel had been working with me to expand my power and Nathaniel had caught us in the courtyard and demanded I go back to my room. Ever since then, Adriel had not been left alone with me. I assumed it was because Nathaniel feared that if my power grew any more, that maybe I could have escaped with the help of Adriel.

Hayes hadn't been brought back to my room either since Devika had brought him to me as a peace offering, not knowing that we shared a rebellious tether. He told me that my mother was glad that I was alive, but we both knew that the real truth was that my mother was happier that I was alive and still within reach of the Imperium.

I could still get close enough to kill the bitch.

I just needed to take out the angels who were in my fucking way.

I'd need to incapacitate Nathaniel first because even invisible, he'd still be able to see me. But I'd also need to take out Cassiopeia, so she couldn't compel me not to strike at Rieka. I'd had a lot of time to think about my plan, and in order to execute it, I needed to assess and plan for all of the League of Dominious' skills.

Verena could cripple me with my fears, even if she wasn't a skilled fighter. Devika could use her pressurization power to crush my brain. Asterin might still be able to hit me with one of her throwing stars even if I was invisible; I wasn't sure if she could ever miss. Makata could turn into any kind of creature so she was an unknown. Draegan couldn't track me when I was invisible so as long as I kept my power up, she wasn't an issue. Then there was Saskia, who would love to fry me alive and Abraxas, whose power was impotent against mine, who both wanted to torture me to death.

The only two people that I wasn't worried about was Adriel, who might not help me, but might not aid his fellow angels as much as they'd like. And Adair, who might be a warrior, yet his healing power wasn't something he could use against me at least while we were actually fighting.

If I could do some recon and figure out when the majority of the major threats were on patrol, then I could find the optimal time for me to strike. I had been fooled by Nathaniel and I was pissed off with myself for letting it happen, but maybe, just maybe, I could convince him that my self-imposed solitude had given me enough time to reconsider my first gut reaction.

It wouldn't be the first time that I had pretended to be all compliant and amenable.

I didn't know how long I was held down in the brig, the time passed by so slowly, and inside the basement level that had no windows, it was easy to lose track of the days. When I had been thrown in here, not for losing my temper and fighting one of the other recruits, but for not stopping when I was commanded, I had fumed and yelled and beat my fists against the bars in temper.

After, when I was exhausted, I'd sat with my back to the wall and my knees to my chest and waited, so eerily quiet that no one would know I was alive if I'd closed my eyes. My throat had burned with thirst and my stomach rumbled from hunger but still I would not give in to the one single command they had issued me before locking me in here: Admit you were weak and secure your release.

But I wasn't about to admit to any weakness.

The door cracked open and I lifted my eyes slowly to the man standing in the doorway. He was a few years older than me, with brownish-red hair that always looked like it was windswept. Blue eyes that usually danced with mischief masked a brilliant intelligence that people tended to forget given his charm. His beard and goatee were the same reddish-brown as his hair, giving him that authentic Irish appearance.

This man told stories like no other and he was the closest thing to a brother that I had.

"Alright, Trouble."

Trouble, the nickname Tiernan Byrne had called me for as long as I could remember. It usually made me roll my eyes, and try and hide a smile but today, I didn't feel like smiling. Tiernan tossed me a hard piece of bread that I devoured before taking the water that he then held out to me. When I was finished, he took the water back and leaned against the wall.

"You'll get in trouble for feeding me."

Tiernan grinned, shoving his hands into his pockets. "Eoghan owed me winnings from a game of cards, told him I'd forget about it if he let me in and had a little amnesia about my visit."

Snorting, I rested my chin in my hands. "You can talk your way in and out of anything, Tiernan. You'll be one of the leaders in no time."

It was Tiernan's turn to roll his eyes. "Well, if that's the case, then listen to me now, Trouble. Do what they want you to do. Suck it up and take the hit. I know, I know it's not in your nature to back down, but we need you out there with us. We work best as a unit and right now, we are down one of our sneakiest assets."

Suspicion coursed through me. "Did something happen?"

"I'll tell ya when you get out of here." Tiernan said as he pushed off the wall and went to the door. "We are due to head out again tomorrow, Raven. You should be with us. Think about it."

And I had, long after Tiernan had left. I wondered if Tiernan was manipulating me at their behest. If somehow, the person I was closest to in the world was just another soldier to them, a tool for them to use against me. If I wasn't such an asset, if I didn't have my powers, would I have even been worth checking in on?

Rebellion and war didn't foster trust in many.

If they had used Tiernan against me in order to get what they wanted, then it was the smartest idea because of all of my unit, it was Tiernan that I would always listen to.

Tiernan was the reason why I swallowed my pride and admitted that I was weak to secure my freedom, the words tasting like lies as I stood there in front of our leaders and gave the appearance of being a perfect fucking soldier.

And I hated myself a little for it.

But just like I had when I had agreed to be Nathaniel's little spy around the citadel, I would have to suck it up and play docile in order to lure Nathaniel into a false sense of security, and through him, the rest of the League.

And then I would start to unravel the bonds that tied them together.

Firstly, I went and showered, dressed in clean clothing, and left my hair loose around my shoulders. I had to use everything in my arsenal to pick away at Nathaniel, and I knew that he was attracted to me, and maybe I could use that as well...I just had to make sure that I remembered what a traitorous prick he was when my body reacted to his.

When I was sure that I was suitably dressed, I gave Grainger another scratch and went to the door, flinging it open. Verena jerked off the wall that she had been leaning on, obviously not expecting me to emerge from my room. She wore a vest top and cargos, like she wasn't expecting to engage in any kind of hostility today, her flame-coloured hair was pulled back into a braid and the veins on the right side of her face seemed to pulse.

Amber eyes watched me suspiciously as I placed my hands on my hips and curved my lips into a smile. Verena blinked, and glanced over her shoulder, her white and amber wings shifting before she said. "Hey Raven, you need something?"

There was a trepidation in her tone that I couldn't fault her for, considering I'd openly challenged Rieka, Nathaniel, and even Verena after it all went to shit. I'd said some horrible things to her, lashing out with my words.

"You know what, Verena? You are a monster who devours people's fears and uses them against themselves. Come on, you want to know what mine is? You want to come and give me a kiss and eat my fears?"

"I was looking to speak to Nathaniel."

Surprised flashed across Verena's face. "You want to speak to Nathaniel?"

"Yup." I replied, keeping my face as nice and neutral as I could.

Verena studied me intensely, and glanced down to my waist as if she was looking for the axe that I preferred to use. Nathaniel, during the first few days after the events in Rieka's throne room, had returned my axe to me, cleaned from the blood I'd drawn from Cassiopeia when I had flung the axe at her in my attempts to get away.

"Are you planning on murdering him?"

Shrugging my shoulders, I told her honestly. "I'm not feeling very murdery today. But tomorrow, that's not decided yet."

The corners of Verena's mouth tugged up, and I knew I had thawed her just a little. Leaning against the door-frame, aware that I was not allowed to step foot outside the room without permission, and I was trying very, very hard to pretend that I was well-behaved.

Verena pulled a cigarette from behind her ear and lit it with a lighter, taking a drag before she replied. "Nathaniel is out on patrol right now. He won't be back in the citadel until later."

"Okay, can you tell him that I want to talk to him when he gets back? Thanks, Verena."

I made to close the door, but Verena stuck her booted foot in the way, preventing me from closing it. Tilting my head, I looked right at Verena as she asked. "What are you up to, Raven?"

Verena's questioning was timid compared to some of the training I'd received, hell, even some of the torture I'd received so pretending that I wanted to be friends with her and even Nathaniel again was a walk in the park.

"I'm going crazy cooped up in here all day. Grainger is cute and all, but other than grunting or snoring, he's not a great conversationalist. If I'm gonna be stuck here for the foreseeable future, I figure that I should bite the bullet and see if he would let me off my leash a little. I have too much fucking energy. At least when I was down in the dungeon, I was too weak to do anything but conserve the sap of strength in case anyone else tried to touch me."

Verena flinched because she was one of the only angels who had seen the emaciated state I was in when

Nathaniel had come to fetch me to be his little gambit. I'd been so weakened that when we had come to the steps that led up to the League quarters, it had taken everything in my power to force myself up the steps.

"If you are too tired, I could carry you." Nathaniel said.

"I would rather crawl on my hands and knees than have you carry me, bird boy."

"Does it mean that you now accept what Nathaniel did to keep you alive?"

What? I thought to myself. You mean when he lied his ass off to get me to do what he wanted and then publicly humiliated me in front of his bitch of a mother. Yeah sure, I totally accepted that.

I eased back from the door, letting Verena step inside as I shook my head. "I'd be lying if I said that I did, and you'd never believe me if I told you I had. Things went down how they went down, but I'm not doing myself any favours keeping myself locked up here. I want to train; I want to breathe in the fresh air and sit in front of the fire and relax."

Verena was still looking at me so I reached out and touched her arm, the angel so shocked when I did and she flinched. I kept my fingers on her bare arm as I told her. "Please, V. I know that I was a bitch and I know that I said some shit, but I spent three years alone in the dark and I don't think I can do it again. Just tell Nathaniel that I would like to speak to him and then it's up to him if he wants to grace me with his presence."

Removing my hand from Verena's arm, I went over to the bed and climbed onto it, laying down on the pillow and closing my eyes as I heard Verena walk out of the room and close the door behind her. I heard voices outside then I heard the sound of a ball hitting the wall and I knew that Verena had stepped off her watch to be replaced by Asterin, who liked to bounce a ball to pass the time.

I didn't want to get too cocky into thinking that I had fooled Verena, but I couldn't help but smile as I closed my eyes and allowed myself to drift off to sleep. I dreamt of being chased down a darkened road, the sound of wings hunting me in the dark and when I peered over my shoulder, hands grabbed for me and I jerked awake with a start.

Grainger had come over while I was asleep, his body was curled up beside me, his wings twitching as he slept peacefully. I pulled the duvet up over his pudgy body and he huffed out a grunt that I was gonna take as a thank you.

A knock sounded on the door. I got up off the bed and went to open it, surprised to see Verena standing there. She didn't look too happy as she said. "I flew out to speak to Nathaniel. He said he is due back at around midnight and I can escort you to the kitchen where he's planning on grabbing something to eat. If that is too late, then he said he could come by in the morning."

Smug delight threatened to spill out to my features and I had to fight against the smile that wanted to curve my lips. "No, midnight will be grand. Will you come get me when it's time? Or maybe we could hang out for a while? If you're not busy that is."

Verena looked surprised, but then she smiled. "I could hang. Or if you want, come out to the hall for a change of scenery and someone will let us know when Nathaniel is back."

This was starting out exactly how I wanted it.

TWO

For a couple of hours, I sat with Verena, with Asterin, and then Devika when she returned from whatever she'd been assigned to do. She kissed Verena on the cheek, then held out her fist to me to bump. The angels stayed within the confines of safe territory, talking about random things being handled around the citadel, careful to keep away from mentioning the Imperium.

I soaked it all in, and unbeknownst to the angels, I managed to get an understanding that right now, Makata and Draegan were on shift with Nathaniel, while Cassiopeia was on site in case of an emergency. I had no clue where Adriel and Adair were. I didn't dare probe to see where he was in case it raised the angels' suspicions more.

I yawned just as an angel came up the steps, her smile almost as bright as her pink hair. This angel was shorter than me, her left wing was misshapen, and while it always seemed to me to be a crime to give someone extremely gorgeous wings and then make it so that she could not fly. Her eyes were big and wide on her small face.

Kalila came forward, stopping just shy of where we were all sitting, and gave a little wave to the members of the League, before she turned her blue eyes on me. "Master Nathaniel has returned and is in the kitchen preparing some food if you still wished to speak to him."

The angel turned and went back the way she came, stopping on the stairs as Saskia came up, dressed like she's been at some party or something, her top so small that her breasts overflowed, and her skirt was so short that if she bent over, you'd probably get a view of her ass. Kalila moved to the side swiftly as Saskia glared at all of them and I was worried she might strike out as Kalila. Getting to my feet in a quick movement, my gaze locked with Saskia and I mentally dared her to come and have a go.

Then Kalila was gone from view, and the three angels that had been sat with me were on their feet beside me. Saskia swept her purple hair off her shoulders, then went into her own room.

I was actually disappointed that I wouldn't get another go at her.

A hand landed on my shoulder and I peered back at Verena. She inclined her head, like me standing up for Kalila was a sign that I had indeed softened to them once again. Little did she know that I hated when people picked on those who couldn't or wouldn't protect themselves. I fucking hated bullies.

Probably why I despised Rieka so bloody much.

"C'mon, let's get you to Nathaniel before he thinks you've changed your mind."

Verena walked me down the stairs and along the corridor toward the small kitchen that the League of Dominious had within this section of the citadel. With every step we took closer, my heart started to race and my chest was tight. I needed to reign in my anger, and my nervousness at seeing him in the flesh after so long. The nights when he'd guarded my room, I *felt* him outside, though he never once spoke. Nathaniel had never taken a day shift, as if it was easier to watch me at night when I might be asleep. But his presence had only disrupted my sleep and made me crankier.

We stopped just outside the kitchen, with Verena turning to look at me, a stern expression on her face, making the veins pulse on the side of her face. "You need his blessing to get back to training, Raven. Don't piss him off just because you know how to push his buttons."

Then Verena was gone, leaving me alone in the corridor and I wondered what would happen if I tried to bolt down the hall and escape. Would someone leap from the dark corners to catch me? Glancing from left to right, I decided that running wouldn't get me closer to the Imperium so I could stick my axe into her dead heart.

Pushing open the door to the kitchen, I strode in and stopped dead. I should have prepared myself for the onslaught of seeing Nathaniel again because despite the fact that he was attracted to me, I was also stupidly attracted to him, my body heating and tightening.

His head was bent over as Nathaniel worked on his sandwich, his inky black hair falling into his face. He wore a short-sleeved black t-shirt that was pulled across his broad chest. As if he sensed me watching him, he straightened to his full over six-foot height and he lowered his lashes, those eyes filled with thunderstorms dipping to run over my body before he went back to making his sandwich.

Nathaniel didn't say anything, in fact, he turned away from me. His obsidian wings shifted as he rinsed some of the utensils he'd used, giving me a little respite as I walked over to the counter and hopped up on one of the bar stools. Looking down at the counter, I saw that Nathaniel had prepared two plates, and my heart kinda stuttered.

When I breathed in, I caught the scent of strawberries and glanced at the concoction in a glass. It looked revolting, with foam and bits of what looked like herbs floating in it, but the scent of it made me want to have a sip to taste it. Reaching over, I wrapped my hand around the glass, held it to my nose and almost groaned at how nice it was up close.

My stomach rumbled and I felt compelled to take a sip. As I raised the glass to my lips, before I could even take a sip, a firm had gripped my wrist and yanked it away from my mouth. Between one second and the next, Nathaniel had ripped the glass from my grasp, but still had his fingers locked around my wrist.

"You can't fucking drink that." He growled at me, not letting go of my wrist when I tried to yank it back.

"Okay, whatever, Nate. Let go of my fucking wrist. I'm sorry I took your stupid drink, okay? Just let me go."

We glared at one another, something tangible in the air that mixed our aggression and lit a match, making the taunt thread between us almost combustible. Nathaniel suddenly let go of my wrist like he'd been shocked, and I slid off the chair and headed for the door.

"Fuck this shit. I asked fucking nicely to speak to you and the first thing you do is growl at me for touching a stupid drink? Whatever."

I was at the door before I heard Nathaniel say my name and I turned, folding my arms across my chest while I glared at him. Nathaniel ran a hand through his hair, reached for the second plate, and pushed it toward the space where I had been sitting. I arched a brow and he sighed, sitting down himself as he motioned for me to come back and sit.

Weighing up the benefits against any ground I'd lose if I walked out the door right this minute, I walked back over and retook my seat. I didn't touch the sandwich he'd made for me, just leaned back in the chair as Nathaniel looked at me.

"I apologize," Nathaniel said after a pregnant pause. "The drink is a medicinal mixture that could potentially have harmed you."

"Are you sick?" I asked, telling myself that I didn't care if he was or not.

Nathaniel snorted, and I could almost swear his eyes

went darker still. "I think you'd like it if I said that I was unwell."

Shrugging my shoulders. "Not at all. I mean, if you were dead, then who knows who would take over my leash? Better the devil you know, and all that."

Nathaniel scowled, glancing at the drink and then back at me.

"Jesus, just drink it, Nate. I promise not to snatch it from you."

As Nathaniel drank his concoction, I reached over and swapped our plates, taking the sandwich he'd already taken a bite from with my uneaten one. He shook his head as he drained the glass and then went over to rinse it out before turning back to me.

"You've reverted to thinking we would poison you?" Nathaniel observed, an accusatory tone accompanying his words.

"Well considering you stabbed me in the fucking back, Nathaniel, do you blame me?"

Nathaniel snarled, lifting his sandwich and taking a bite, chewing it with his jaws so tight that I thought he might dislocate it. I ate my own snack, then pointed at the jug of water. "I'm okay to take some of that, right?"

When Nathaniel didn't respond, I rolled my eyes and instead went to the pantry, came back with some orange juice, and poured myself a glass, setting the jug on the counter. We said nothing for another few minutes, but my curiosity got the better of me.

"Well, other than the obvious, what's wrong with you?"

Nathaniel glanced away, and I could almost swear that his cheeks were tinged with red like he was embarrassed. He rubbed the back of his neck, before turning back to me.

"It isn't something I wish to have public, and it wasn't something I ever wanted to have to try and explain, especially to you."

There was a lot to unpack with that statement and I wasn't sure where to start.

"You don't have to tell me. It's grand. It's not like we are best buddies or anything. Forget it."

"It's embarrassing." Nathaniel grumbled and I couldn't help but laugh.

"For fuck sake, Nathaniel. You've literally seen me covered in my own filth and beaten half to death. It can't be more embarrassing than that."

He's quiet for the longest time, and I know that in his head, Nathaniel is debating whether or not to just be truthful with me. If it was me, I would be considering that us sharing this secret, whatever it was, might give him a stronger foothold and be a tentative step in a better direction than we'd been heading these past few weeks.

"I'm not sick." Nathaniel told her but said no more.

"That's good?" I mused, framing it as a question and Nathaniel barked out a laugh that had my skin pebbling.

"I think you'd prefer if I was unwell." Nathaniel stated, though his tone was teasing, some of the tension easing from his body.

"Then I couldn't actively try and get on your nerves to see you react because I might just feel sorry for you."

I was surprised at how easy it was to shift into openly loathing him, to this exchange of banter that felt too easy, too familiar. I had to remind myself that I should be home right now, back with my family and friends, and not locked away in this citadel as the Imperium's pet human.

"The mixture is an herbal medicine attuned to my physiology. I didn't know what it might do to you if you drank it. It's something I used to drink while I was with Saskia in order to prevent a pregnancy."

I blinked in surprise. The drink was Nathaniel's way of making sure he wasn't stuck with the sparkly bitch through a child? I was acutely aware that he was watching me to gauge my reaction.

"Because an Imperium's reign can continue through a child and if Saskia was the mother of your child, that would give her as much power as being Imperium herself."

Nathaniel inclined his head. "Exactly. I had one of the apothecaries prepare this and I developed a taste for it. It's just routine to drink it now."

"So, drinking it still doesn't mean that you are hooking up with the apprentice bitch your mother likes?"

"Fuck no." Nathaniel ground out, then he seemed to catch himself, his gaze turning to pure molten heart as he smirked. "That's a very pointed question for someone who professes to hate me."

I can feel my cheeks heating but I let loose a snort. "No, it's the question of an astute person who needs to know if you've let your cock rule your head and decided that fucking Saskia would be a great way of releasing some tension."

"You mean like you told Devika you would do with that human boy? Michael?"

Fuck, fuck, fuck...It had bothered Nathaniel so much that he had made a point of learning Hayes' fake name. I had to warn him at the first possible opportunity, and get him to make it clear that he and I were nothing but friends.

"That's a very pointed question for someone who professes to hate me." I tossed Nathaniel's words back at him and he frowned, his nostrils flaring and his wings shifted.

Letting loose a sigh, I rubbed at my chest, Nathaniel's gaze dropping to where my hand rested on my bare skin and I felt a thrill lick along my spine. "I think it was smart to protect yourself from Saskia. It sounds like a trick she would use in order to keep you close. But I don't think I've seen any angelic children around the place. Are there baby angels in Ireland?"

Suspicion crossed over Nathaniel's expression and anger surged in me.

"For fuck sake. It was an innocent question. What do you think I'm gonna do, Nathaniel? Do you think I'm going to sneak into a nursey or something and slaughter innocent angel babies? What kind of monster do you think I am? No wait, don't answer that, I can guess."

Getting down from my seat, I shook my head, the rage I'd tried to keep contained inside me boiling and simmering in my veins. I wanted to throw something at his stupid head and make him bleed. I wanted to punch and kick and scream at him.

"Raven, wait."

I can feel him coming to stand behind me, the heat of his body making my palms itch to reach out and touch his skin. Reigning in the impulse, I faced him, folding my arms across my chest and jerked my chin up.

"I didn't mean to infer that you might harm an angelic child. Angelic pregnancies are unpredictable and we must keep the children safe, at all costs as they cannot protect themselves. Back home, it is not unprecedented for a couple to try for decades to welcome a child."

And yet it had only taken one rape to produce me.

"I would never hurt a child, angel or human. I might be a Rebel but even I wouldn't sink that low."

Nathaniel ran his hand through his hair, leaving it standing at odd angles. It made me want to laugh, but I kept my features guarded, waiting for Nathaniel to make the next move.

"Verena said that you wanted to talk to me about getting back to training with Adriel."

I tried to ignore the hint of jealousy in his tone as I nodded. "We can only do so much in my bedroom." Nathaniel's lips curved into a snarl and I rolled my eyes. "I really want to punch you. The room is too small for him to fully flare his wings and let me fight him from below. After Aramis, I need to learn how to get hit by a wing and not let it derail my momentum. If Adriel hits me enough times, my body will adjust to the pain and I'll get desensitized to it."

Nathaniel appeared pensive for a moment. "How many times have you done such an exercise to get desensitized to pain?"

I tried to remember the number of times, but I lost track counting and then decided to give Nathaniel a little bit of honesty in the hope that he would be more agreeable. "You know, I don't remember them all. Too many probably. My friends would say that me being so fucking stubborn helped with the training."

"Well, that's a statement I can vehemently agree with."

I was so shocked at the droll tone that I laughed, rolling my eyes. "Fuck you, Nate."

Nathaniel grinned at me and it changed his features from brutally harsh to brutally beautiful. It was as if the past few weeks had been erased and we had slipped back into this weird sort of friendship that I couldn't explain or put a name to. It did, however, make me feel uneasy.

Shifting my balance from one foot to another, I shivered, wishing I'd worn something over my vest. "So, can I train with Adriel again?"

"If you meet the same terms as before. Meals with us. Then you can have access to Adriel to train, access to the library, and the privacy in your room. I am amenable to anything else if I can see that you are trying once more."

I frowned pretending that I was mulling over his

offer. "Then the same rules need to apply as before, Nathaniel. You keep Abraxas, Saskia, and your mother away from me. If one of them so much as looks at me funny, I can't be responsible for my actions."

"I remember. Poor impulse control."

There was an ache in my chest at the stark reminder of the bargain we had once struck, one that Nathaniel had ripped apart when he agreed to Rieka's need to keep me close, because I'd been too fucking useful.

Gritting my teeth so that I wouldn't snap or say something that would set me back, I reminded myself that getting close enough to Rieka to kill her was the only goal I had to work towards. I would sit down and eat with them, train with them, and work to unravel the bonds that tied them together.

This was just how betrayal started...Not with big lies, but with small secrets.

I offered Nathaniel a grin, and watched the surprise in his eyes as I asked, "Does this little meal we shared constitute as a meal and mean that I can train with Adriel tomorrow? Or do I have to wait until after everyone has seen me at the dinner table?"

Nathaniel was thoughtful for a moment, then he turned and went back to the counter. "I'll offer a show of good faith. I'll tell Adriel to meet you in the courtyard tomorrow morning. Do not make me regret this, Raven."

THREE

True to his word, Nathaniel had Adriel waiting for me when I ventured down to the courtyard. The only angel I could assuredly call a friend, the scarred angel who held within him a darkness that mirrored my own. It called to me from our very first meeting and Adriel was the only angel that I knew had no ulterior motive.

His dark hair was mussed, longer than it had been the last time I saw him, the strands falling into his eyes. The scars that marked his flesh were almost hidden and had I not known the emerald shade of his eyes, with his scars hidden, you could almost mistake him for his twin, Adair. But there was no hiding the pulsating power that seemed to be held at bay by sheer force of will.

When Adriel first started to train me, it was something I had noticed but not paid any attention to. Now though, after months of working while being in his presence and seeing the flare of emotions that unleashed his power, I couldn't go back to thinking of him as any other angel.

"You are late."

I laughed, brushing a few strands from my face as I shrugged. "I'm fucking early and you know it. It's not my fault you seem to relish getting up at stupid o'clock to train."

"You complain too much, Raven."

"Fuck you, Adriel. Anyone would think you were eager to beat me up."

Something flashed in his dark green eyes and I cursed myself. "Hey, I was messing. I am fully aware that I'm the one who suggested this to you weeks ago. You are the only one I trust to do it, Adriel."

Adriel gave me a curt nod, then came toward me. "I asked Adair to come by in case you need to be healed. No arguments with this, Raven, or I will put a halt to this little exercise."

I held up my hands to show Adriel that I wasn't going to argue. "Okay, but can I just point out that I need to get injured and fight through it in order to get used to it without you feeling bad? If Ascian has more Seraphan in the citadel, they won't wait for Adair to heal me before they try and kill me. Just saying."

Adriel mumbled too low for me to hear him but I had no doubt he was cursing me. I strode to the middle of the courtyard and lifted my face to the sky. Rain trickled down and it was icy cold as it hit my skin. It was on the tip of my tongue to ask Adriel if an angel's wings became sodden in the rain the same way as a bird's when I felt a wing slap against my back.

I hissed as I whirled round to see Adriel's wings flared out, spanning out from his back, the green bleeding from his primaries into his secondary features. I had a second to admire his wings before one of those wings was coming toward me, and I braced for the impact.

The slap of the wings against my chest had me sucking in air as pain roared in my sternum. I wheezed out a breath, the pain making me dizzy. Adriel beat his wings upward, hovering in the air as I tried to concentrate, my entire body screaming as Adriel whirled and smacked his wing into me again.

A scream wrenched from my throat and I went down on my knees. It fucking hurt like hell to take a breath and I was sure that Adriel's wings had broken a rib or two. Gritting my teeth, I slowly got to my feet and faced him, wiping sweat from my brow. "Again."

I lunged for Adriel before he could think about it too much or I could let the pain cripple me like it wanted to do. Out of reflex, Adriel kicked out at my already injured ribs, yanking the air from my lungs and making my head spin as I ran right at his legs, hoping to force him to land.

Adriel shot upwards, beating his wings and forcing the wind to beat at me until I landed on my ass. I rolled away as he came downward, trying to stamp on my already damaged ribs. I groaned, forgetting to duck at the last minute due to a dizzy spell and Adriel's wing hit me hard in the face.

It was like being hit by a fucking truck.

I landed awkwardly, hitting my head on the concrete and it knocked me out cold.

"Raven."

I turned toward the voice, and saw my mother standing in the doorway to my room in the barracks, her expression stern as I wiped the tears from my face. "I'm sorry."

She came to sit on the end of my bed, and reached out to tuck my hair behind my face. "There is nothing to be sorry for, Raven. Tiernan told me that if you hadn't of fought off the savages from the wastelands, then he might not have gotten the supplies we needed so desperately."

"But now they all know that I've been pretending to be weaker. They might find out what I am."

My mother shook her head. "I told them that I was training you a little more than the others. As a mother is entitled to do with her only child. It's the reason you have excelled. And when faced with losing a person that you care for, something snapped in you. Tiernan might not have made it out without you."

Cupping my cheek for a second before she rose, my mother turned to me. "I know that I am not the most affectionate person, Raven, but I do love you. Everything that I have done is to protect you and our secret."

"Mam?" I groggily said as I felt a hand on my head and then I groaned, nausea rolling in my stomach. I lurched to the side and vomited on the ground. My vision was blurry, and I was wheezing, my lungs feeling like they were rattling.

"I think I broke her ribs, Adair. I can hear how hard it is for her to breathe."

"Ya, I can feel it. I need to sort her head wound first. I think she has a concussion."

"She can hear you both," I mumbled, as I felt Adair place a hand just under my breastbone and it fucking hurt for a moment before there was a blast of heat that felt so nice that I leaned against the ground and moaned, the nausea started to rescind.

After a few minutes, I was breathing normally again, and Adair had taken his hand off me. I went to sit up, my vision swimming still, and I think I might have fallen over if Adair hadn't put his hand on my shoulder to steady me.

"Fuck, that hurt." I said, as I lifted my gaze to where Adriel was watching me with a veiled expression.

Closing my eyes for a few minutes, I took in a few hesitant breaths, and when it didn't hurt any more, I got to my feet, with Adair standing close enough to grab me if I keeled over. Rolling my shoulders, I took the water that Adair handed me and drained it, not giving a fuck if it was poisoned or not.

"Thanks." I said to Adair, then turned to where his twin was staring daggers at me.

"What the fuck is eating you?" I snarled at Adriel, setting my hands on my hips.

Black bled into his eyes for a second before they returned to their natural colour. "I could have fucking killed you."

I placed two fingers over the pulse at my throat. "Still alive. Let's go again."

"Are you completely insane?" Adriel asked me, nothing but pure ice in his tone.

I flashed him a feral grin. "Probably. I should have ducked when you aimed your wing high to avoid getting hit in the face. I'll remember next time. C'mon, Adriel. Let's go again."

Adair was watching the interaction, though he didn't say anything until Adriel asked him to outline just how much Adriel had injured me. Adair glanced at me, and I shrugged, knowing Adriel wasn't going to get on with things until Adair did as his twin asked him.

"Two broken ribs that could have punctured your lung. Bruised sternum. Fractured cheekbone and eye socket. Concussion and a ruptured blood vessel from when your head hit the concrete."

Lifting my hand to my eye, I touched my hand to the bone. "That's new. Don't think I've managed to get any injuries to the eye before. Well, apart from a dozen or so black eyes."

Adriel is still looking at me and I can't understand why this time me getting injured bugs him so much. "Adriel, I'm grand. You've hit me just as hard when we've been sparing. It kept me alive when Aramis attacked me. I asked you to intentionally hurt me. I'm not angry."

"I'm bloody angry, Raven." Adriel growled, his fists clenching and unclenching. "You stand there all glib about the fact that I broke your ribs and ask me to do it again like it's nothing. Do you not realize what it takes from me to hurt you? Before you were just someone to spar with who did not look at me like I was damaged, but now, I car-"

My heart clenched as Adriel snarled and turned away from us. I looked at Adair and mouthed to him to go, as I walked around Adriel and reached out and gripped his arm. He shuddered under my touch, and I could almost feel the darkness in him reacting to me.

"Hey, it's okay. I get it. I remember being shocked the first time the closest thing to a brother I had broke my baby finger so I would know what the pain was like. I didn't understand how someone I cared for could do that to me, but he explained to me that doing so was protecting me. It's exactly what you just did and what I hope you'll continue to do. Because I care about you too, Adriel."

I gave his arms another squeeze before I let him go. Adriel was looking at me with a tenderness that looked foreign on his face. Something bigger was happening to Adriel in this moment than I could put into words, as the angel lifted his hand and touched the cheek he had fractured.

His eyes were focused as if he expected me to flinch at his touch. There was nothing romantic or sexual in his touch. No, instead there was this careful brush of fingers that held the promise of protection, of a kinship that transcended race, gender, or bloodline. What had started out as two creatures coming together with no judgement, had moulded into something akin to what I had with Tiernan, what I had with James, and even Hayes.

"I always wanted a sister." Adriel said softly, his fingers still on my face.

"Even one with a death wish like me?"

Adriel chuckled, still touching my face, like it was the first time in a long time he had dared to touch someone so gently in case he might hurt them.

"Am I interrupting something?"

Adriel yanked his fingers from my face as he turned to where Saskia was standing with her hands on her hips. She looked from Adriel to me, then back at Adriel. The smirk on her face told me that she had seen Adriel touching me and believed it to be seedier than it was. I wanted to punch the smirk off her face for it.

She was obviously heading out somewhere on patrol, wearing leggings and a thin vest top, a toned-down look from her usual slutty attire. Her hair was pulled back off her face into a bun, her purple eyes gleeful.

"Does our commander know that you were touching his property, Adriel? I'm not sure he would be best pleased to know that the two of you were out here gazing lovingly into each other's eyes."

"Get lost, Saskia. I'm sure you've got to be skanky somewhere else."

Electricity danced over her fingertips. "I will fry you where you stand, you fucking rodent."

Lifting my hand, I beckoned her forward, flashing her a toothy grin as she took a step forward. Adriel snarled a warning, but I wanted to best her for a third time and show her up even more. I knew it had to be eating at the sparkly bitch that she had been beaten by a pesky human twice before, not that she knew I was just a little bit more than a normal human.

Adriel stepped in between us, looking at Saskia. "Go, Saskia. I have little patience to deal with you today."

"I don't take orders from you, Adriel."

"But you do take them from me."

I jerked my head to the right to see Nathaniel walking into the courtyard with Adair, having moved so quietly that I hadn't heard him, but from the look on Adriel's face, he had indeed heard Nathaniel and his twin approaching.

"You are late for a shift, Saskia. Go and relieve Verena."

Saskia looked like she wanted to argue, and whatever she saw on Nathaniel's face made her swallow hard, then flare out her wings, crouching as she flapped her wings and took to the skies. Nathaniel waited until Saskia was nothing but a blur in the distance before he came over. He looked between me and Adriel. "Is everything alright?"

"If you don't count the sparkly bitch's appearance, we're all good." I told Nathaniel, watching as his lips twitched as he tried to hold back a smile.

"How did the training go?" He asked, his gaze narrowing when he looked at Adriel, who glared back in turn.

"Oh for fuck sake." I all but growled, feeling annoyance at the way in which Nathaniel was reacting. "Adriel was worried that he'd almost killed me and I was trying to get him to stop being stupid. It had worked until sparkles showed up and now you. But I'm not stupid."

Turning to Adair, I folded my arms across my chest. "You mind tagging along the next couple of sessions in case I break my ribs again?"

Adair looked to Nathaniel. "I have sentry duty tomorrow morning at this time until evening."

I glanced over at Adriel. "You good to do a nighttime session tomorrow? I mean, it might be good to train in the dark as well because your wings will be almost untrackable in the dark."

Adriel looked like he was going to argue with me, then he saw the resolve in my face and just sighed. "Best that it be me, I suppose, considering you'll find some other fool to beat you up if I refuse."

I mock punched him in the arm. "That's the spirit. Now, if you're not gonna beat up on me some more today, I'm going to have a nice hot bath and then hang out in the library before dinner." I lifted my gaze to Nathaniel. "Dinners still at six, right?"

"Yes. We will see you there. Adriel, a word before you go."

Hesitating, I kept my feet firmly where they were until Adriel gently nudged me with his shoulder. "Off you go, Raven. We will see you at dinner."

Tossing Adriel a fuck you expression, the angel laughed as I made to head inside, halting as I said to Nathaniel. "Don't be a dick to him."

"I'll try not to be."

Satisfied that I had done everything I could to

prevent the two angels from fighting, I gave Adair a quick incline of my head, before proceeding to my room. I spent a few minutes scratching Grainger's tummy, then went in and filled the bath. Stripping off my clothes, I got in and almost sighed at the nirvana of the warmth against my flesh.

Closing my eyes, I submerged myself under the water, replaying Adriel's attack over and over until I could start to figure out where I should have ducked, where I should have pivoted to avoid a block or blunt the impact.

Once I was all blissed out, I got out of the bath and towel-dried my hair, reminding myself I needed to wrap a towel around me because of Grainger. I dressed quickly and then just like I said, made my way to the library, where I scoured the shelves for a book to read, purposely avoiding looking for any of Nathaniel's journals.

Selecting one from the right side of the bookcase, I went over to the floor, right in front of the fire, lay on my back beside the heat, and opened the book. In this book, in a dystopian not all that dissimilar to my life, the world is under the grasp of a ruthless ruler, and as I continued to devour the story, I feel a kinship toward the heroine and her sacrifice to keep her sister safe.

I would have done the exact same thing as Katniss did to keep my family safe.

The fire crackled beside me and I shifted closer to it, setting my book down for a moment as I stared at the ceiling. I needed to up my game and start to work toward getting to Rieka. I'd played nice today and would have dinner tonight. I wanted to see how far I'd get around the citadel before someone caught me. I also needed to get a message to Hayes that he was on Nathaniel's watch list.

I wasn't best known for my patience, but I would wait a few days before I dared an attempt at slipping free of my guard. I was aware that even though they didn't stay outside my room that I was still under scrutiny from the angels while the trust was rebuilt.

I just had to wait until I was sure Nathaniel was not in the citadel before I went snooping. Then the game would be afoot and I felt the thrill run through me at the idea of getting one over on the angels.

FOUR

I was surprised by how easy it was to slip into old routines with the angels. Every evening I had dinner with the League, then Adriel either continued to teach me how to play chess, or I watched him and Nathaniel play, sometimes for hours. I trained with Adriel as often as possible, and he started to get me to spar with the other angels so that I could get used to different strengths, and different fighting styles.

Wanting to know everything, I asked Adriel if some of the angels could use their powers against me, so I could learn to fight through it. He refused without offering an explanation. He'd also eased up with the force of his blows with his wings when he hit me. I could tell the difference, but I didn't say anything in case it put a halt to our training completely.

Most nights after dinner I hung out with Verena or Devika, whoever was off duty. It looked like Nathaniel always made sure there was an angel off duty that I could hang with. He probably assumed that having an unofficial babysitter would keep me out of trouble.

Like that was gonna happen.

Nathaniel was missing one night at dinner, as was Adriel, Adair telling me that the two angels were on the night sentry duty, and I knew this was my best chance to get out and snoop around a little and hopefully, get to Hayes.

After dinner was done, I waited until I had yawned a couple of times, then got up off the floor in front of the fire, waving off Verena when she made to follow me.

"I'm good, V. I'm gonna crash. I'm exhausted."

Verena looked like she wanted to push, but Devika put a hand on her arm, unspoken words between them. I offered a goodnight to the room, then headed straight back to my room in case anyone decided to check up on me. Climbing under the covers, I feigned sleep until I heard the angels retire for the night.

Leaping out of bed, I put on a long-sleeved back top, then put pillows in the bed to make it look like I was still sleeping should someone pop a head in to see if I was still in my room. Grainger lifted his head to look at me, then grunted before closing his eyes again, ignoring me.

Releasing the hold on my power, I felt it slide over my skin. I listened to Adriel when he told me that a power was just like another muscle. In order to make it stronger, it had to be used, it had to be strengthened. The more I used it, the stronger it became. At first it was hard because I had spent most of my life hiding the full extent of my power, however, Adriel had been working with me to extend my range, and focusing my power on making certain things invisible. Yesterday I had managed to keep my axe invisible while I stayed visible, but the moment Adriel had hit me with his wing, the pain made me lose concentration and my power slipped.

Shrouded in my power, I gently pried open the bedroom door and peered outside. I wasn't surprised to see that while I might have been given some leeway and freedom, Nathaniel didn't trust me enough to completely rescind my jail wardens.

But considering I was about to do something sketchy and sneak out, he was probably right.

Devika was sat on the window ledge, Verena in between her legs and they were oblivious to anyone around them. Dev's legs were wrapped around Verena's waist, her head thrown back as Verena kissed down her neck. Verena had her hand up Devika's top and as they kissed, their moans mingling as Verena slid her hands under Devika's ass and walked them toward their bedroom.

The moment the door shut behind them I was out of the bedroom and down the steps before another angel came to watch me. I hurried down the corridor, a giddy feeling in my veins as I passed by the open door of the library and heard voices. Looking in through the gap of the open door, I saw Eliseo and Hannele.

I had met Eliseo, an angel who could garner the history of a person or an item with just a touch, one of the first times I'd gone to the library. He wasn't like other angels, his power giving him an aversion to touch.

Hannele and Eliseo were brother and sister, and Hannele could understand any language written or spoken. I'd made note of it because the Rebels had made a point of re-establishing the Irish language as a means to communicate, and if Hannele could understand it, humans needed to be careful when speaking to one another.

"I do not like the girl in my library. She takes the books down and does not put them back in their places. Everything has a place, Hannele."

"I think if she knew that every book has a place, that you had it organised in such a way, then she would be more careful. I can have Kalila have a word with Raven."

Oh shit, they were talking about me. I'd caused Eliseo discomfort because I'd just put my finished books into any empty slot. Guess he had a system I was messing up.

"And the pages...Kalila must tell her about the pages."

I heard the amusement in Hannele's tone. "Of course. Perhaps if you gave her one of your lovely bookmarks, then Raven might not turn down the pages of the books to mark her place."

"We will see if she returns the books to their right places before I give her a bookmark. We cannot give nice things for wrong doings."

I bit down on my lip to stop from laughing, but I'd definitely make a more conscious effort to put the books back where I found them. I left Eliseo and Hannele to their Raven bashing and strode down the corridor, halting when I heard the sound of someone hitting a target in the courtyard.

Backtracking, I strode to the open doors to see Abraxas training alone. I always considered it to be ironic that the monster who loved to torture people looked the epitome of how the human world viewed angels before we came face to face with them. With snow white wings that gleamed in the darkness, his hair was the same white, and the palest blue eyes I had ever seen, Abraxas seemed like he was as pure as driven snow. And yet, if you looked at his eyes for a prolonged period, you could see the glimmer of evil and wrongness in that angel.

"You think that's bad? I'm just getting started."

I shuddered at the memory of the gleeful tone Abraxas had used when the Imperium had given him permission to torture me some more. I could see it in his eyes, how every scream, every gasp pf pain, every broken bone had given him a hard on. Abraxas liked violence and I knew from seeing him with Saskia that sometimes, violence and sex were one and the same.

I thanked my lucky fucking stars every day that Abraxas had decided not to indulge in the latter with me.

Nathaniel had told me that Abraxas was also one of the angels who had deflected to Ascian's leadership. He wore the evidence of his betrayal with the handprint burn mark at his throat. Nathaniel had also rebelled, but his mother had granted him the mercy of marking him on his chest where he could hide it.

Abraxas was using a wooden contraption to practice his punching. I wondered why he was training all alone and why none of the League were here, but maybe they too saw the wrongness in Abraxas and decided to stay well away. I hated him with a passion, almost as much as I hated the Imperium.

Maybe I should have some fun with Abraxas and mess with his head.

Grinning as I walked over to the weapons rack and picked up one of the kendo sticks, the weapon becoming invisible as I stretched out my power. This had been easy for me to learn, because the weapon was connected to me by touch and Adriel thought it was because a weapon was an extension of me.

I stalked Abraxas, waiting until he lifted a leg to kick a target and I snapped out the kendo stick, hitting him on the back of the thigh and he faltered. His gaze darted around, looking for his attacker, then he shook his head and went back to his workout. I twirled the kendo stick in my grasp, waiting again until Abraxas punched out and I raised the stick, bringing it down as hard as I could on his shoulder.

Abraxas howled in pain as he staggered forward, then whirled around, a snarl on his lips. Feeling brave and probably a little cocky, I stood beside Abraxas and rotated my hands, holding the kendo stick to the side before I smacked it sideways, catching Abraxas right in the chest.

"Son of a bitch." He growled and I laughed, the sound carrying in the dead of night. The growl that came out of Abraxas' chest was inhuman. "I fucking knew it was you. Make yourself visible and let's have a fair fight."

Nothing with Abraxas would ever be a fair fight and we both knew it.

As he steadied his stance and braced for another attack, I couldn't help but use one of the moves, Adriel had shown me and swept the kendo stick to the back of his ankles and Abraxas went down on the concrete with a grunt, his knees hitting it that was sure to have rattled his teeth.

"I will kill you. I will cut you into tiny little pieces and feed you to those creatures in the wastelands. The League can't watch you every goddamn minute of the day and night. I'm coming for you."

Striding over to the weapons rack again, I pick up one of Asterin's throwing stars. Angling my body so Abraxas wouldn't know my exact location, I tossed the kendo stick at him, the white-haired angel catching it with ease but now his hands were otherwise engaged. Without a second thought, I flicked the throwing star out of my grasp and it embedded in his shoulder, right where his hands had rested before he had dislocated mine.

I was already jogging out of the courtyard as Abraxas roared my name, cursing me. Oh, it had been a long time since I'd had so much fun. The grin on my face was so wide that it hurt my face, but I didn't care. It made me wonder if I could mess with Saskia like I had with Abraxas.

With my fun done and dusted for the night, I made the decision to head down to the human servant quarters and I practically skipped down the corridor. I took in some of the patterns of shifts from the angels milling about the citadel. I noted who seemed to linger near the servant quarters and who looked at the humans heading down into the basement area with hunger.

Fucking predators.

I stayed by the door that led down the stairs for about half an hour, a steady stream of humans coming and going and that prevented me from finding a gap to slip down the stairs and find Hayes. I had to hope he was still in the citadel because I hadn't seen him in a while. The flurry of movement finally started to ebb and I waited until a young girl left the door open as she carried a tray downstairs, giving me an opening.

Surging forward, I crossed the corridor, ready to duck inside when hands gripped my shoulders and yanked me inside a pitch-black room. I immediately reacted, punching out but my aim was blocked by a muscular shoulder. I brought my knee up to aim for the groin because I knew my attacker was male, but that move was also blocked, a thick thigh now in between my legs.

My heart was hammering in my chest as a hard male body was pressed up against me and I knew, I fucking knew that it was Nathaniel's thigh between my legs, his hands roughly gripping my arms. I jerked in his grasp, his thigh rubbing against me and I had to bite my lip hard to not moan at the sensation.

"What the fuck do you think you are doing?"

I blinked my eyes a few times to adjust to the darkness, his features coming into focus. Oh, he was pissed as hell with me. His breath was warm against my skin, his hands warm and I wondered how much of it was down to Nathaniel himself and how much was the fiery power contained inside him.

"Playing hide and seek. Oh look, you found me."

The growl that came from deep in Nathaniel's chest made the hairs on my body rise and I shivered, holding his gaze in bold defiance. Nathaniel rested his forehead on mine and we just stayed that way for a few minutes, like he was trying to get a hold on his temper.

"You can let me go now." I said quietly, Nathaniel's grip only getting tighter, bruising so.

The hand that was gripping my arm gradually eased to run up and down my bare arm and I sucked in a breath. Part of me wanted to arch into his touch, to touch him like he was touching me, and yet, something with more common sense than my body told me in the back of my mind that if I touched him in the way that I wanted, it would unfurl something neither of us could take back.

"I trusted you to behave."

"No, you didn't," I remarked with a snort. "Or else you wouldn't have stationed guards at my door to keep me in check."

"You lied to me." He snarled in response, his hand slipped down my body to rest on my hip. His lips brushed against my temple and it stopped my fucking heart. His anger, it was vicious and cutting, though he had no reason to be angry with me. His rage reached out as if searching for my own, and stroked it like it was a lover and I reached my hands between us, placing my palms on his chest and shoved him hard. But Nathaniel had dug his heels in, and couldn't be moved.

"Not so fucking nice when someone lies to you, is it?"

His nostrils flared but he didn't respond for a spell and then I heard him say softly. "Rieka would never have let you leave."

"Rieka wasn't the one who offered me a chance to see my family again and then claim to be clever with words to trick me."

"Rieka," Nathaniel said with a snarl in his tone. "Would have had you killed. She would have made Adriel kill you. If not Adriel then she would have made me just to make her point. That she is in control. She has felt my opposition to her tactics of late and she would have used you to pull me back in line. I am the commander of the League of Dominious and I must protect them from her."

I knew all this...I'd heard it all before...didn't make his betrayal any less fucking hurtful.

"You could have gotten me out. You could have dropped me off in the wilderness and forgotten all about me. But you chose to keep me here as her pet human."

"You may not believe me, but my actions were to protect you, Raven. As long as my mother thinks I have bowed to her will, she will humour me my rebellions, and my Rebel."

"I'm not your bloody Rebel, Nathaniel." I hissed at the possessive tone he had used when saying my Rebel. "We will always be at opposing ends."

His forehead is still pressed against mine, his hand on my hip squeezing as he sighed. "Maybe not always, Raven. The world has shifted before and it may shift again...sooner than we both think."

"Ya, right..." I retorted, rolling my eyes. "I'll believe that when I see it. The only way that we humans want to see the world shift again is for you fucking monsters to go back home and leave us the hell alone."

As suddenly as he had grabbed me, Nathaniel lets me go and I instantly miss the heat of his body. My heart is pounding so loud that I can feel it pulsing in my head. I draw in a few shaky breaths. "I take it you'll be dragging me back to my room now like a Neanderthal?"

"Raven, lose the fucking attitude." Nathaniel snarled, his hands glowing slightly and giving me a quick look at his face, and I could see the hurt in his eyes.

"I wouldn't have a fucking attitude if you weren't such a dickhead." I countered, unable to stop myself from goading him.

"You know what?" Nathaniel said with an icy tone. "Do what you want, Raven. I watched you needle Abraxas. I saw how much you enjoyed it. I can't keep trying to ensure your safety when you are hellbent on testing your mortality."

Hope blossomed in my chest. "So, you'll let me go?"

"No. That is the one thing I cannot do."

I laughed, a harsh and bitter sound as I let my power slide away. "You know I had planned on walking down those stairs and just watching the humans but now I think I'll go introduce myself. I'm gonna go speak to my own race for a while. So, you can stay here and mope if you want, Nate, or you can go fuck yourself. I'm done. I'm so fucking done."

Yanking open the door, I startled a human who was

walking by and she looked into the room, yelping as she spotted Nathaniel and then looked at me. Her cheeks heated as she no doubt thought I'd been up to something scandalous with Nathaniel.

I glanced haughtily over my shoulder, ignored the heated glare from the commander, and turned back to the girl. "Definitely not worth the five-minute trigger. I've had better."

Nathaniel didn't so much as respond to my taunt, and I didn't look back as I boldly walked over to the door to the servants' quarters and descended down the stairs, about ready to throat punch someone.

T he moment I got to the bottom step, I instantly felt self-conscious as the entire hallway seemed to freeze at my sudden appearance. Most of the humans in the citadel knew each other and they did not know me... and as Rieka's pet human, I could understand the look of suspicion on their faces.

"Can I help you?"

I turned to see an older woman glaring at me, my gaze dropping to the kitchen knife in her hand. I'd have no issue with knocking it out of her hand with the untrained way she held it, though I was trying to not alienate my own people, so striking an old woman probably would not help persuade them that I was still one of them.

"I was looking for Michael."

The woman glanced at a girl around my age, jerked her head up and the girl rushed off as more and more people ducked their heads out of closed doors to get a glimpse of me. I sat down on the bottom step and rested my chin in my hands as I waited, humming the melody of *The Fields of Athenry* while I waited.

The song made me smile, because any time Tiernan had too much to drink, he'd burst into old Irish anthems that he'd learned as a boy. He sang them so much, even us younger kids had them imprinted in our brains.

The older woman was still watching me, her eyes trained on me. None of the others came forward, and it looked as if the woman was the defacto leader of the kitchens. When a group of younger children peaked out from one of the rooms, she barked out a command and they all disappeared back into the room.

Ten minutes passed and I was still sat at the bottom of the stairs. It made me wonder if the humans had a secret exit and entrance down here. I knew I'd have to ask Hayes, if he bothered to show up. The girl that had been sent to fetch Hayes come back and she was breathing hard. The older woman bent down low and the girl whispered something in her ear.

The older woman straightened, slipping her gaze back to me. "Well, Michael will be along shortly, but you might as well come in here for a tea. You're only blocking the stairs sitting there."

Shoving off the bottom step, I walk into the kitchen area and take the seat the old woman points to. In the light of the kitchen, I can see the faint glint of grey in her blonde hair. She went over and filled the kettle, then set it on top of the stove.

"I believe you are Róisín's girl."

"If I say yes, will you promise not to hold it against me?"

The woman snorted, the kettle whistling as she filled the mugs she had gotten out of the cupboard and brought them over to the table and sat down across from me. I added milk from a jug on the table and took a sip, sighing. "It's been so long since I had a decent cup of tea."

"I'll make sure to stock some in the League's kitchen for you." The woman said drolly, and I just took another sip of my tea.

"How do you know my mother?" I asked the woman, smiling at the occasional inquisitive face that peaked in to catch a glimpse at me.

"Everyone knows your mother, child."

That was a masterful evasion of my question and I lifted my mug in a show of respect. We sat there sipping our tea, the woman scrutinizing me thoroughly. I heard boots coming down the hall and while they didn't sound like Hayes, they did seem achingly familiar. Setting down my mug, I got up off the chair, and turned to face the young woman who rushed into the room.

Tall with brown curls and brown eyes, Aoife Lynch came to a halt when her gaze landed on me, those eyes going wide as she pulled down the hood of her cloak. The last time I had seen Aoife, when I was at the angelic party and I had tried to follow her, it had been a glimpse of the girl I had grown up with.

"I didn't believe Hayes when he told me you were alive. But you are."

"Apparently, I'm hard to kill no matter how many times the angels try. It's good to see ya, Aoife."

We'd never really been close, and if it had been Tiernan or James, I'd have hugged them, but Aoife was looking at me like I was the enemy and I didn't like it one bit.

Blowing out a breath, I yanked up the hem off my t-shirt and turned so she could see my back and all the scars. I heard Aoife gasp and I dropped my tee to face her again. Her eyes softened, and then she strode forward, hugging me to her. I closed my eyes to stop the wave of tears that threatened to spill out.

Aoife let me go then, and I stepped back as she ran her gaze over me. "I'm due to go home tomorrow and I'll tell everyone that I've seen you. When we got word that you were alive, it took orders for the leaders to stop Tiernan and James from coming to get you. Tiernan's face is too well known by the angels for him to dare coming to the citadel."

"Stupid idiots would get themselves killed. I'm safe enough for the moment. Tell them I'm doing everything I can to get home to them. But not before I finish what I started."

"The commander has you on a tight leash, girl." The older woman interrupted.

"Molly, leave her be." Aoife said, but I put a hand on her arm.

"He does. But he also knows that my sole purpose is to kill Rieka. I tell him often enough that it has to have sunk into this stubborn head by now."

"You speak of him with such a familiarity, child. Should we Rebels be worried that the lines between friend and foe are blurred?"

Laughing, I slumped down on the chair again. "Nope. Nothing to worry about. If it wasn't for the fact he can see through my powers, I'd have acted already. I speak of him with such familiarity because in order to best my foes, I need to know everything about them. So, I watch, and I learn and I plan."

The woman inclined her head as a young boy came in and tugged at Aoife's cloak. She turned to me. "I've got to go. But I'll see you soon."

"Tell the other idiots to stay well away. I'll see them soon enough."

Aoife pulled up the hood of her cloak, and was gone before I could even blink. I slumped down in my seat and closed my eyes. I must have drifted off to sleep because I felt a hand on my shoulder and I reacted. Grasping the hand that was on me, I jumped up and twisted it, getting a yelp of pain and my eyes focused on Hayes.

"Jesus fucking Christ, I would have killed you, you idiot."

I let go of his arm, and Hayes rubbed it gingerly. "My mistake. You always were cranky when woken."

"Fuck you, Hayes." I said with a chuckle, looked to see Molly, the older woman still in the kitchen.

"The commander is stalking the corridors above. Does he know that you've come down here?"

"Of course he does. I told him I was coming down here after he caught me sneaking about. We argued and he told me to do what I wanted so I came down here. He probably thinks I've found the first male I could find and jumped his bones. It's whatever."

Hayes swore as I looked at him. "You might want to stay far away from him because not only does he know Devika brought you to my room, but he knows your fake name too."

"You've painted a target on my back, Raven! How the fuck am I supposed to gather information if I have to keep an eye out for the angel who clearly thinks of you as his?"

"You may not believe me, but my actions were to protect you, Raven. As long as my mother thinks I have bowed to her will, she will humour me my rebellions and my Rebel."

"I'm not his and don't use that tone with me, Hayes. I don't belong to you either. I'm actively working to drive a wedge between them all and to do that I have to get real close. You are as bad as he is if you think I'm going to stand being a possession."

Hayes rubbed his temples like I was giving him a headache and maybe I was. I was giving myself a bloody headache as well. He leaned against the counter, a scowl on his face. "The angels will kill you if they figure out you're trying to pit them against one another, Raven."

"Way to state the obvious. I goddamn know my life is in constant danger. I'm surrounded by monsters who want to kill me. Do you know how lonely that is? Do you? Because while you are down here, laughing and living with your own kind, I'm stuck up there fighting to stay alive. So take your bullshit and shove it right up your ass, Hayes. I'm done."

The chair scraped along the floor as I surged to my feet, thanked Molly for the cuppa, and took the first step before I felt a hand grip mine. Wide eyes looked at me as I turned round and sank down on the step again, holding the gaze of the boy who was about twelve or thirteen.

"Can you really go invisible?"

I grinned, nodding my head. "Wanna see?"

The boy nodded eagerly and I pulled my magic to me, and reached out to tap the boy on the nose. The boy giggled as I made myself visible again, a stupid infectious grin on his face.

"That's so cool."

A crowd gathered again as Hayes and Molly came out of the kitchen. Hayes' eyes were dark and filled with something I didn't want to think of as I ruffled the kid's hair and headed up the stairs.

"Raven."

I glanced down at Molly as she said. "Tell me about the angels."

I was aware that I had a captive audience and I could tell that Molly wanted me to not sugar coat anything from the youngsters who might be as intrigued by a mutt who could go invisible as they might be with an angel who could do them harm.

"You want to talk about the angel's, let's talk about the fucking angels. They are as beautiful as they are cruel and if you let them in, if you let them fool you that they care about you in the slightest, they will eviscerate your soul. They will be exquisite to behold, but they will poison your heart if you let them. They are soldiers in the guise of beauty and they are bred for destruction. They will make you think they are your friends but then they show you just how insignificant you are in their vast immortality. And when they..."

And when they eventually kiss you like you fantasize about, you already know that it will be like you finally caught a glimpse of the sun and it burned you from the inside out.

Shaking my head at the thought that ran through my mind, I opened the door and I could feel Nathaniel's presence like the battering of a storm. I looked back down the stairs, ignoring the weight of Nathaniel's glare. "But most of all, kids, just remember that angels are just massive dickheads. And that ends Raven's lesson for today."

I closed the door with an audible snick and strode passed the angel who had obviously been waiting out here all this time. He fell into step beside me, his wings brushing against my shoulder in a deliberated way, and I suppressed a shiver.

"You know, you can be a real bitch sometimes."

I barked out a laugh. "Shocking as it may be, that's not the first time someone has told me that."

Nathaniel laughed, the sound like a rumble of thunder. I smiled to myself before I remembered the interaction in the darkened room, then I ground to a halt and turned to Nathaniel. "What game are you playing, Nate?

You get mad at me and now you've done a one eighty and we pretend we are friends again?"

Nathaniel leaned against the wall and folded his arms across his chest, the muscles on his arm flexing. He arches a brow when he catches me looking, and I arch mine right on back, daring him to comment on it, but he doesn't.

"What will we achieve if the two of us are constantly at each other's throats? I can tell you all day long that what I did was to protect you, but I think with you, actions speak louder than words. I need to show you that I care about your safety for you to believe it. And while I think it was reckless to goad Abraxas, I'd be lying if I said that watching you didn't amuse the hell out of me."

I blinked in surprise, then tried to cover it by looking at his lower half and before I could stop myself, I'd already committed to it. Lifting my gaze to Nathaniel's I tried to ignore the molten intensity in his eyes.

"What?" He asked, his tone gravelly.

"I was looking to see if someone had removed to stick up your ass while I was downstairs."

Nathaniel pushed off the wall with a roll of his eyes. I jogged to catch up with him, then stopped to look out the window at the angels flying over the citadel. I leaned my elbows on the ledge to get a closer look, the array of colours like a rainbow of feathers against the black of night.

Long before my mother had told me that I had angel blood in me, I had always been fascinated by wings. I wanted to know what it would be like to take to the skies and soar above the world below. Once, when I was like five, Tiernan had found a set of dress up wings and hoisted me above his head and twirled me around and around like I could fly.

I'd felt the wind on my face, felt the joy in my heart. Then my mother had found us and the next day, my mother told me that I was part angel, part monster and I never put the wings back on again.

"What just ran through your mind? It's the softest I've ever seen you look."

Part of me wanted to keep the sliver of my past to myself, but maybe I was just too tired of everyone seeing me as either a monster or a possession, that I just wanted to be seen as me...as Raven.

"As a child, I was so fucking fascinated by angels' wings, I used to collect feathers of all different colours when they fell from the sky. I'd wanted to know what it was like to fly. My brother gave me dress up wings and I pretended I could fly like an angel."

"How old were you?"

I titled my head to the side as we came to the end of the stairs leading up to the bedroom. "Five or so. My mother wasn't happy with me and I never wore the wings again. I still collected the feathers, but in secret after that. I still have them in a box under my bed. Well, I think they're still there unless all my shit got thrown out when everyone thought I was dead."

Nathaniel is staring at me now, and me at him as he reached over his shoulder and plucked a feather from his wing and held it out to me. "For your collection."

"I can't take that." I told him even as my fingers reached out to take it, our fingers grazing as I took the feather in my grasp, felt the silkiness of it, committed the feel of it to memory.

Nathaniel shrugged. "It would have fallen out the next time I took flight. It was already loose. Since I cannot let you go home to see if your collection is still there, let me help you start a collection here. Goodnight, Raven."

He strode up the steps two at a time, leaving me standing there with my mouth open. I stroked the feather along my fingers, and sucked in a breath. Fuck, fuck, fuck. This was not part of the plan. Nathaniel was supposed to continue being a massive dickhead and make it so much easier to hate him. The gesture was sweet and thoughtful and it reminded me of the angel from his journals.

"When the man who wrote in that book wants to come and have a word with me, come see me."

I'd said that to him in the aftermath of what had happened with Aramis. I'd given him a way in and Nathaniel had used it. The feather in my grasp was proof of that. I should have said nothing, I should have kept my secrets and my heart guarded.

Feeling unsettled and unbalanced, I climbed the steps to my bedroom, stopping outside Nathaniel's room, and I wondered what he would do if I opened the door and went inside. Hell, what would I do?

I burst into my room, got a grunt of annoyance as I shut the door behind me and leaned against it, my abrupt entry having disturbed my roommate. I lifted the feather and looked at it, the obsidian colour even more vivid up close. It made me wonder what the rest of Nathaniel's feathers would feel like under my fingers and I hated myself for it.

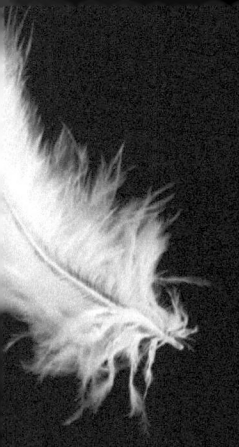

My bare feet slapped against the stone as I bolted through the never-ending corridors of the citadel. Thunder rolled outside, followed by the deafening crack of lightning that speared through the darkened skies. The wind seemed to be in a frenzy tonight also, whipping my hair against my face, hard enough to cut. I scented blood in the air and knew it was my own.

And more of my blood would spill this night.

The sleepshirt I wore didn't shield me from the elements, nor did my exertion heat the blood in my veins. I was cold, so fucking cold. Terror was a hard fist in my stomach. A clap of thunder startled me and I stumbled over my feet, slamming hard into the wall and I felt something tear in my shoulder.

Once I had a grasp of myself again, I ducked down a narrow pathway, having to turn sideways to fit through, and found myself in the dungeons. I couldn't be captured down here, for if I was, they would surely chain me up and yank the chain every time that they needed my abilities.

I hurried up the stone steps with no finesse or coordination, using my hands as well as my feet to ascend. Bursting out of the door, I paused to get my bearings, trying to clear the panic from my mind so that I could figure out how to escape the monster who stalked me.

My heart was beating so loudly inside my chest, I was sure that the monster could hear me and track me that way. Was it thrilled by my fear? Did it enjoy the hunt as much as it seemed to?

I heard a snarl of impatience and took off down the hall, not daring to chance looking over my shoulder to see just how quickly the monster hunted me. I could feel its presence, like a warm breath on the nape of my neck, ready to capture its prey.

Heading back in the direction of the place where the chase had begun, I burst through the doors of the courtyard, into the wind and rain, trying to locate a weapon to defend myself. The rain pelted down on me, soaking my skin, leaving my hair sodden and loose around my shoulders, and sticking to my flesh. I wiped the hair from my eyes, my heart sinking at the lack of weaponry in the training area.

It was as if I had been herded into a space that I knew down to my marrow, had hoped would help me against the monster, but I stood alone, defenceless, and marked for death.

Something landed by my feet and I looked down to see a feather of blue and white lying in a puddle. Then as I lifted my gaze to the skies, feathers of all colours, of all sizes and textures fell from the sky in tandem with the rain. I twirled around as the feathers drifted to the ground, falling softly around me.

Angels beat their wings, fighting a battle in the sky, faction against faction, League against Seraphan. The cries of war were as loud as the thunder that boomed and the lightning that pierced through the sky. It was devastatingly beautiful, the flash frame of the images and had I been artistic, I might have wanted to paint it from memory, immortalized for all to see.

The doors to the courtyard shattered, glass and wood splintering and I had to duck to avoid being impaled by a fragment. I braced myself for attack, knowing that against this creature, I'd never be able to fight them off. But I would not go down easy. I was ready for war and war had come banging on my door.

The monster loomed in the doorway; its eyes trained on me. A vicious snarl curled its lips, flashing teeth at me. Its hands were clenched into fists and I wondered if it uncoiled them, would claws be there in place of fingers that had once touched me with a tenderness that had made me ache.

"You lied to me!" It roared; the sound of his indignation almost drowned out by the rumble of thunder.

"I had to." I admitted to it, hoping that somewhere deep inside, the monster might understand why I had to keep my secrets.

Reaching behind its back, the creature withdrew a sword, the metal becoming alight with flames. It was then that I could make out its features, even now, moments before my death, I was struck by how strikingly beautiful the monster from my nightmares was.

His inky black hair glistened with dampness, his storm-filled eyes raging as much as the storm around us. Sharp *cheekbones and a chiselled jaw that I knew felt scratching to touch. His chest was bare, the mark of his rebellion on show for all to see. I had thought that he might understand, that he might sympathize with my plight, with my curse, but the moment he realized that I had lied, I saw my death in his eyes and there was no way to talk myself out of it.*

The flames on his sword danced a hungry dance, like they hungered for the taste of my flesh and were eager to sate that hunger. I looked from right to left, searching for a chance at survival, for a friend to come to my aid and save me from certain death.

But I was alone...there was no one coming to save me... and I could not save myself this time.

"I know what you are."

Frost in his tone, I shifted my gaze back to Nathaniel, my shoulders slumped. "I know."

Between one breath and the next, Nathaniel stood before me, the heat of his flames almost scorching my skin, but it was the heat of his gaze that threatened to burn me from the inside out. His free hand reached out and gripped my chin with a bruising grasp so I couldn't look away.

"I want to hear you say it. I want to hear it from your own lips. What are you, Raven?"

For a moment, it seemed like the entire world fell away and it was just me and Nathaniel left, not even the weather dared to interfere as I wet my lips and told him. "I'm a Nephilim. I'm half angel."

He growled at me, the fingers on my chin tightening. "A filthy half-breed with deceit in her blood. You fooled us all,

Raven. And now I will put an end to your pitiful existence. And if you needed any proof as to why we are monsters, this will surely be enough..."

Nathaniel shoved me away, angling his sword a second before he struck, the blade going into my abdomen, but I felt it in the fragments of my heart. Fire licked at my flesh, the pain searing me as I went down on my knees, my eyes never leaving Nathaniel's as my flesh burnt and he raised the sword, one final time at my neck...

I screamed into the darkness, jerking up in the bed. Feeling disorientated, I heard a snuffle as the scream kept coming, my throat burning as the door to my bedroom burst open and I screamed louder still as the Nathaniel from my dreams bled into my waking life. He strode forward. "Raven, it's just me. Tell me what is that matter."

"I want to hear you say it. I want to hear it from your own lips. What are you, Raven?"

Nathaniel crouched down in front of me and reached out to touch me.

"Don't touch me. Don't fucking touch me." I scrabbled off the bed to wedge myself into a corner. Hugging my knees to my chest, I stayed there frozen in fear as the tendrils of the nightmare wove terror into my bloodstream.

"Should I get Adriel?" I heard Devika ask Nathaniel, and realized my screams must have alerted the entire League that I was losing my shit.

"No." I managed to croak out. My hands fumbled

looking for wounds, and I was almost relieved to not feel any blood seeping where I had felt the blade sink in. My skin was hot, like the flames had followed me from my dreams, and I was acutely aware of how close Nathaniel was to me.

Lifting my gaze to Nathaniel, I felt my pulse quicken, in fear as I said. "It was just a nightmare."

About you...

I didn't need to say the words, and yet Nathaniel immediately understood. His expression seemed hurt, but I couldn't deal with his feelings right now when I was trying to smother my own.

"I'll stay with her, Nathaniel."

I wasn't sure if having the angel who could garner my fears with a touch was any safer than having Nathaniel around, but I had a feeling that no one was going to let me spend the rest of the night alone. Staying where I was, I listened to Nathaniel and Verena's conversation.

"Her fear is so pungent; it woke me up. I don't know what nightmares haunted her, but most of the time, I can't sense a lick of fear from her. She's shielded better than anyone I know save Adriel. But tonight, her shields were shattered completely from that nightmare. I hate to say it but she is terrified of you."

"I wouldn't fucking hurt her, V." Nathaniel snarled, glancing back over at me and I flinched, I couldn't help it.

"Then maybe you should stop glaring at her when she can't help her nightmares. I'm sure she's got more than a few."

Placing my fists over my eyes, I pleaded in my head for them all to just leave me alone. I heard a grunt. Followed by a heavy weight on my knee. Reaching out as I opened my eyes, I patted Grainger on the head as he unfurled his stone wings and mimicked my patting with a there, there sort of action with his clawed hands.

Despite how bleak I felt, I couldn't help but laugh at Grainger's attempts to comfort me. After a few minutes, he hopped off my knee to fly back to the desk, curled up, and went back to sleep. Pushing off the ground, I walked back over to the bed and climbed back under the covers, though I remained in an upright position, pulling the covers up over my chest.

Verena took out her lighter and lit a candle, the flames dancing with shadows and I jerked my gaze away, the feeling of my skin on fire forcing bile up my throat.

"I've got her. You can check on her tomorrow."

Then Nathaniel was gone, sucking all the tension from the room with his departure. Verena closed the door and came to sit on the end of the bed. She didn't say anything, but I did see her rub her temple.

"I'm sorry if my shitty nightmare woke you."

Verena smiled; her amber eyes filled with understanding. "It's grand. When we first brought Adriel home, his fear and his nightmares kept me awake for weeks. It was so strong that I was actually sick and then one day, he just shut it all off, like he'd found a switch in his head and there was this void of emotions. You can be like that sometimes."

I really wished there was a switch inside my mind that I could turn it all off with.

"Hey, I'm okay now. You can go back to bed now and leave me to my embarrassment of waking the citadel with my girly screaming."

Verena leaned back on her hands. "When I was younger, I hated my power. I'd always wanted to have a cool power that would get me into the League of Dominious, but became the angel everyone was afraid of. I'd step into a room and a prisoner would piss themselves at the sight of me and I'd done nothing but enter a room."

I remembered how hard it was for me as a child, with my power and knowing that I was one false step, one wrong word from certain death, so I listened to Verena speak, interested to know what had happened to her.

"My mother was like Adair, a healer, and my father was a teacher. They did not know what to do with a child who could reduce a grown angel to tears when she was annoyed and used her power against them. Angels refused to touch me, even as a child, because everyone has a fear."

"That seems very harsh."

"It made me stronger. I had to be to join the lower ranks of the League. It was hard, because no one wanted to train with me. No one wanted to risk my touching their skin in case I saw their fears. But then a young shy angel asked me to spar with him, because he too had a different cross to carry."

My heart stuttered a little at how Verena described

Nathaniel as shy, and yet I had to make sure that was who she was referring to. "Nathaniel?"

Verena nodded her head, a warm smile on her lips. "As the son of the Imperium, trainee soldiers didn't want to fight royalty. His mother was a member of the League also, so he was doubly cursed. But I was glad to have someone to spar with, someone I could call a friend. I'd never had a friend once my power made itself known."

I knew how that felt.

"Anyways, when it became clear that Nathaniel might one day lead the League, he made sure to bring people into our little group that would be strong and fierce in battle, but loyal to the League. The only angel he didn't select was Saskia; that was all Rieka's influence."

I snorted, brushing my hair from my face. "See that makes a lot of sense. I couldn't see Nathaniel choosing her as part of his League."

"As much as you ruffle his feathers, Nathaniel was never hard until after the rebellion. He will always be the angel who made the League let me touch them so they would know that I knew their fears, and they had to trust that I would never use them against them. It's how the League can freely touch me now because we have an unbreakable trust that I will not break."

I didn't know if I had it in me to have that sort of trust in someone. To hand them over my fears and my secrets and expect them to still care for me. As much as someone carrying the burden of what I was could trust. I had often wondered what Tiernan or James might say if I told them I was a Nephilim after all this time.

Would it crumble the sisterly affection they had for me?

And Hayes, would it make sense to him why I'd been so cold after we'd had sex? That I had felt absolutely nothing during those moments and I had always wondered if it was because of the tainted blood in me.

I already knew that Nathaniel would kill me for my secrets.

I shivered and Verena lay across the end of the bed, resting her chin on her hand. I regarded her for a moment, wanting to know if she had picked up anything else from my nightmare but decided against it. There was no point in alerting her that there might be more to the story than a terrifying nightmare.

"Is that how you met Dev? When she joined the League?"

A dazzling smile crept over Verena's lips. "Ya, I wasn't expecting her. She was the first after Nathaniel to offer to show me her fears and the only one to even ask me what mine was. When I told her that I was afraid of never finding someone to love all the parts of me, Devika kissed my cheek and told me that she could tell that I had a good heart and any angel would be lucky to love me. It happened gradually, falling in love, but I think I fell in love with her that very first time. She loves all the parts of me."

"If I was a romantic, I'd gush and tell you that was very sweet, so can we pretend that I did instead of being the cynical bitch I am?"

That made Verena laugh, then roll her eyes. "Even I

know how sappy I sound. But it's only with her. No one else."

She rolled off the bed and stretched out her limbs. "The drench of fear is gone now. You want me to go or would you rather I stay a little longer?"

"I'm not gonna lie and tell you I'm gonna go to sleep, but I'm good. Thanks for staying."

Verena smiled and headed for the door.

"V?" She turned to look back at me. "What was Nathaniel's greatest fear?"

Verena had already told me that she wouldn't betray the League's fears, but I had to ask, I had to know.

"A person's fear changes over time. His greatest fear as a young soldier is not the same as it is now."

"And now, what is he afraid of?" I prodded, a deep-seeded need in me to learn the truth of his fears.

"I won't betray his trust. It's been a time since I felt his fears, but if you were Nathaniel, what would you be most afraid of?"

The answer struck me like the lightning in my nightmares.

If I was Nathaniel, I'd be afraid of becoming like his mother.

"Goodnight, Raven."

Then Verena was gone, leaving me alone with my thoughts. I considered my plan to pit the angels against one another and my first intention had been to try and split Verena and Devika up. How could I do it now that Verena had told me the story of them? How could I take away that bond and not feel like a monster myself?

I lay my head down on the pillow, closing my eyes but all I could see was Nathaniel plunging his sword through my gut, and I felt the flames try and consume me. I tossed and turned for what seemed like hours and I was glad that when I fell asleep, I did not dream.

I was still exhausted as I dragged my ass to training a couple of hours later, yawning as I entered the court-yard and unable to stop the replay of the dream in my head as I stood in the same spot that Nathaniel had killed me in my nightmare.

"I know what you are."

Frost in his tone, I shifted my gaze back to Nathaniel, my shoulders slumped. "I know."

Between one breath and the next, Nathaniel stood before me, the heat of his flames almost scorching my skin, but it was the heat of his gaze that threatened to burn me from the inside out. His free hand reached out and gripped my chin with a bruising grasp so I couldn't look away.

"I want to hear you say it. I want to hear it from your own lips. What are you, Raven?"

For a moment, it seemed like the entire world fell away and it was just me and Nathaniel left, not even the weather dared to interfere as I wet my lips and told him. "I'm a Nephilim. I'm half angel."

He growled at me, the fingers on my chin tightening. "A filthy half-breed with deceit in her blood. You fooled us all, Raven. And now I will put an end to your pitiful existence. And if you needed any proof as to why we are monsters, this will surely be enough..."

Nathaniel shoved me away, angling his sword a second before he struck, the blade going into my abdomen, but I felt it in the fragments of my heart. Fire licked at my flesh, the pain searing me as I went down on my knees, my eyes never leaving Nathaniel's as my flesh burnt and he raised the sword, one final time at my neck...

Shaking my head as if it will remove the nightmare from the darkened corners of my mind, I look around expecting Adriel to join me or snipe at me for being late when I was in fact early. Thankfully, it wasn't raining, or that would have been too much of a sensory overload that might have just scrambled my brains even more than they already were, though there was a muggy kind of heat that felt heavy.

I rolled up the sleeves of my top and with no one to spar with, I went to the weapons rack, gathered up a few blades, and walked over to Asterin's target board. Each blade was a different weight and size. I flipped over a small dagger in my hand, catching the handle, and tossed it at the target. The blade wedged into the wood. I picked up another blade and did the same, the repetitive movements calming me.

Once I'd thrown all my blades, I went over and pulled

them out, then did it again. Over and over until I felt the fog in my mind clear. Closing my eyes, I smiled, taking in a breath, as I shook my limbs and let myself just be in that moment.

I suppose it said a lot about me that throwing sharp things at wood was a stress reliever.

"Now that's a sight to give an angel a hard-on. If I'd known you'd liked blades, I'd have fucked you with one to your throat when I had the chance."

Snapping my eyes open when I first heard his voice, I spun around to face Abraxas, took in the glint in his eyes, and knew I was in trouble. Abraxas was standing next to the weapons rack and in order for me to arm myself, I'd either have to turn my back on him and hope I got to a knife before him, or risk running toward him to get myself a weapon that I could cause more damage with.

A smug smirk curved one side of his lips, and in his pale blue eyes I saw the same expression that I had when he had tortured me. If I let him see my fear, then it would only excite him even more.

"How about you let me grab a blade and I shove it up your ass and see if that still gets you off if that's what your kink is?"

"My kink is you bleeding to death while I fuck you."

"Ew, hard pass. Even before I found out you were a necrophile, I wouldn't have touched you with a ten-foot pole, Brax. But now it makes sense that you like corpses. I mean, Saskia, right?"

A snarl rumbled from his chest, his pure white wings snapping out as he took a step forward, and I in turn, took a fraction of a step back, inching toward the target. Abraxas narrowed his gaze. "I owe you payback for what you did last night."

I kept my expression blank. "I have absolutely no clue what you are talking about."

"You think you are so fucking clever."

"I don't think it, I know it." I retorted with a cocky grin on my face. "I could outsmart you even sleep-deprived, and wounded. I suspect that if you didn't have such a unique power that the League wouldn't even bother keeping you about. Tell me, Abraxas, does the handprint still itch from time to time, remind you that you're just another fool in the Imperium's net?"

Grinding his teeth together, a muscle in his jaw ticking, I saw Abraxas try and hold back his rage and fail, though he didn't move to advance on me. That didn't mean that he wouldn't attack me, but rather that he was waiting for me to get complacent, expecting me to think that one of the other members of the League would come to my aid.

I laughed, the same taunting tone I had used last night and that seemed to snap his control. With a roar Abraxas beat his wings to hover off the ground, flying toward me and I ran in his direction, dropping to the ground and sliding under him, getting me closer to the weapons rack.

He snapped his wing down, striking me in the sternum and I hissed at the pain but rolled away when he attempted to do it again. I grabbed a sword in one hand and a chain in the other. Abraxas was still in the air as he flew at me. I swung the chain, hitting him in the wing and he tilted sideways from the blow.

I swung the chain again, but Abraxas caught it in his hand, landing on the ground as he yanked the chain, dragging me closer. Letting go of the chain, I slashed at him with the sword and he jumped back, but not before the sword slashed across his stomach, the coppery scent of his blood filling the air.

Abraxas didn't make a sound, but he did press his hand to the tear in his t-shirt, where blood seeped from the wound. Lifting his fingers to his mouth, he licked at the blood and I must have made a face because he lifted those artic eyes to mine. "Your blood will taste so much sweeter."

I braced myself, bringing the sword up parallel to my chest. "Then come at me, Abraxas. Come and try and bleed me if you think you can."

Dropping the chain, he lunged for me, hoping to grab me with his bare hands. I side-stepped and yanked my power over me, as Abraxas let loose a scream of frustration, his eyes darting around the courtyard trying to spot me. His fists clenched and unclenched at his sides, as I stalked around him, before I kicked him in the small of his back and he lurched forward.

"I'm going to smash your skull on the fucking ground until your brains leak out. I'm going to slice into your chest and then feast on your heart. Then I'll take your head and put it in a box and give it as a gift to Rieka."

I circled him, wanting to laugh at his utter frustration but knew I'd give myself away. Abraxas concentrated, like he was trying to find a pattern in my movements. His nostrils flared as his lips curved into a smile once more. "Or maybe I won't kill you just yet. Maybe I'll drag that human boy you seem to be fond of up to my bedroom and make you watch as I break his body? Did you know that it was possible for an angel to break a human's pelvis with one hard thrust?"

Revulsion and rage clawed at me, wanting out as I became visible. I dropped the sword with a clang and launched myself at Abraxas. I pushed him to the ground and punched him square in the jaw, felt the bones fracture but I felt no pain. I straddled his waist, striking him over and over, blood splatting my face as Abraxas laughed and grabbed my face in his hands and brought his head up to mine.

Pain speared through my head, then Abraxas rolled us, trapping me underneath his bigger frame. His thick thighs pinned me to the ground, his arousal hot and hard against my stomach. Abraxas back handed me, splitting my lip as I spit blood at his face, clawing at his face with my nails. He struck me again, then held my hands to my chest, holding them with one hand as he leaned down, his rancid breath on my skin. He flicked his tongue across the seam of my lips, groaned as I struggled against his grasp.

"Keep struggling. I like it."

To put emphasis on this, Abraxas rolled his hips and moaned, and I tried to keep the sudden wave of panic spearing through me hidden, so as not to fuel his arousal.

Last night I had been utterly terrified of Nathaniel as the monster from my nightmares when I should have taken the threat of Abraxas more seriously. His smirk was sinister.

"I think I'll have another taste. Kiss you. Claim you. It will piss Nathaniel off and he will know that every time he even thinks about kissing you, I've tasted you first."

Abraxas leaned down once again but this time, I lifted my head up and he thought that I was making it easier for him to kiss me. At the last minute, I jerked my head and bit down hard on his jaw, not letting go until I tasted his blood in my mouth.

"You fucking bitch."

He pulled back his fist and I jerked my head again at the last second before he could punch me with a fury that might have killed me. His fist went straight into the ground. "Fuck!"

His scream rang out in the courtyard as Abraxas shook his hand out, then let go of my hands so he could rip my t-shirt with his free hand, exposing my breasts. My heart drummed inside my chest as he shifted his body lower down on mine and I had to try hard not to vomit.

Closing my eyes, I ordered myself to stay still, not give him any satisfaction and I drowned out the noise and the feel of his hands on my body. I told myself that I was somewhere else, anywhere else, and then suddenly the weight of his body on mine didn't feel as much anymore.

It's only then that I realize that Abraxas is no longer

on top of me. My eyes dart open and the sky looks grey and ominous above me. I try to roll over to my side, but my body protests. I take in a few gulps of air, feeling someone crouching down beside me and I shrink into myself.

"It's me."

The moment I heard the sound of Adriel's voice, I grab for his hand and he lets me take it, though I know it must cost him something to let me do it. He helped me to sit up, let me lean against his shoulder as I take stock of what is happening around me.

Nathaniel had Abraxas pinned to the wall, his wings melted to the brick and the moment my brain realized that the scent in the air was the scent of Abraxas' charred wings, I had a second to shove away from Adriel before I threw up. My body started to tremble and I felt Adriel tracing circles between my shoulder blades to comfort me.

I tried to pull the remnants of my top around me, wanting to cover myself up in case any of the rest of the League came to witness my humiliation. It was my fault. I knew I should have stayed invisible but my temper had gotten the best of me when he threatened Hayes.

"You went against my orders, Abraxas. I warned you last night what would happen if you sought retribution for how Raven showed you up last night. You fabricated a rouse to draw Adriel away, knowing that I too was away from the citadel."

I watched as Nathaniel growled, then put his palms on each wing and fire jumped across them, Abraxas screaming but he remained fixed to the wall as Nathaniel strode over and crouched down in front of me. "Did he...?"

I knew what he was asking, and I shook my head. "Not yet. He was about to."

Nathaniel's face was a mask as he lifted his gaze to Adriel. "Will you fly out and bring Adair back. And get Verena here so she can make sure no one tries to free Abraxas."

Adriel's hand stilled on my shoulder and I knew he was torn between wanting to look out for me and getting his brother so that he could heal my wounds. The mental scars would stay with me for as long as I lived.

I tilted my head up to see the fierceness in Adriel's eyes, a flash of black. "I'm okay. I never thought I'd say this but I'd very much like your brother to heal me."

Adriel kissed the top of my head and then he was up, and in the air a second later. I shivered at the gust of wind his flight had caused, a chill in my bones. Nathaniel slipped his jumper over his head and held it out to me. "Take it."

I pulled it on over my head, only wincing a little at the pain and I inhaled the scent of Nathaniel in the jumper. When he offered to help me to my feet, I accepted the hand he held out, his jumper swamping me as I stood and I giggled. "I look stupid."

"I think you look fetching wearing my clothes."

That made me laugh again, when the adrenaline in my veins suddenly depleted and I swayed. Nathaniel scooped me up in his arms and I cried out then my face bumped his chest. I heard wings approaching, as Verena dropped from the sky, landing to take in her surroundings.

"What the actual fuck happened?"

"Later." Nathaniel growled, the vibration of it against my skin. "Make sure no one frees him. I will deal with him after."

Nathaniel carried me back to my room, and lay me gently down on the bed, positioning me in an upright position. I made to take off his jumper, but he shook his head. "Keep it."

"God, I feel so dirty. Can I shower, please?"

"Let Adair heal you first. Unless you want me to hold you upright while you shower."

I rolled my eyes. "You just wanna see me naked. I don't think I'll look very attractive with all my face smashed in."

"I think you still look beautiful."

Our gazes locked and I swallowed hard. There was too much in his words that I didn't want to digest and was so glad when the door opened and Adair came in with Adriel. Adair came forward and Nathaniel slipped off the bed to give him more room.

"We have to stop meeting like this, Adair. People will talk."

Adair barked out a laugh, shaking his head. "Then stop thinking you're invincible, if you wanted to hang out, we could have a drink like normal people. Now, shut up and let me heal you."

I chuckled, then groaned as Adair put his hand to my

sternum, then his other one on my face. I must have passed out because when I opened my eyes, most of the pain was gone and I just felt grubby. Adair ruffled my hair as he slid off the bed and went over to Nathaniel and Adriel.

"She needs rest and food. I'll come back and check on her later." Adair touched Adriel on the shoulder. "Why don't you go get her something to eat?"

Adriel looked directly at me, and I nodded. "I'm gonna shower and then I could eat. Will you get some of those little chocolates for Grainger?"

"Of course."

Then the twins were gone leaving me alone with Nathaniel. I got off the bed, gathered up some clean clothes, and padded across the floor to the bathroom, leaving it slightly ajar so Nathaniel wouldn't burst in at the slightest hint that I might have collapsed or something. I scrubbed myself until my skin was raw and dumped all the clothes bar Nathaniel's jumper in the rubbish.

I dressed in comfy clothes, then slipped Nathaniel's jumper back on over and walked back out of the bathroom. Nathaniel's face was unreadable as I climbed back into the bed and pulled the covers over me.

"When I saw him on top of you..."

"Please...don't...not right now. I can still feel his hands and his lips on me, and I can't think of what might have happened or I won't be able to function." I told Nathaniel, surprised when he came to sit on the edge of the bed, forcing me to shift so he could sit closer to me.

Nathaniel reached out to cup my cheek, the feel of his hand heating the chill in my bones. I didn't want to remember the feel of Abraxas' lips against mine, I wanted to erase it.

"I don't want my last kiss to be his. I don't want him to have that power over me."

I didn't ask him; I didn't say the words but Nathaniel knew what I was not saying. "Close your eyes."

It was one of the only orders I didn't buck against, my heart racing as I felt the warmth of Nathaniel's lips pressed softly against mine. I committed it to memory, knowing I could never let myself be this vulnerable with him again. His lips were warm against mine and it felt like rush of blood to my head.

A knock sounded on the door and we broke apart, Nathaniel on his feet and looking away from me so I couldn't see his expression but I heard the waver in his voice as he said. "That'll be Adriel with the food. I'll be back soon."

EIGHT

I lifted my fingers to my lips as Nathaniel ducked out and Adriel came in carrying a tray of food and what looked like a mug of tea. Adriel set the tray on the side and plucked a chocolate from the side, taking it over to Grainger. The gargoyle grunted his thanks and I smiled.

Returning to the tray, Adriel came over to the bed, walking to the other side as I leaned against the headboard. He set the tray in my lap, then perched himself on the bed beside me, his wings tucked tightly against his back.

"You'll squish your wings."

"They will be fine. Eat something. It might be a long time since I have used my powers to heal, but I do remember that a body needs energy in order to replenish."

I glanced over at Adriel, his face drawn into a pinched expression, his hands in his lap. He had his legs crossed over at the ankles, his dark hair tumbling down and curling around his ears. The faint hint of day that came in the window lingered on his tanned face, making it look darker.

"Eat, Raven. Or else Nathaniel will come back in here and feed you himself."

Rolling my eyes, I picked up a sandwich and bit into it. "Happy now?" I said around a mouthful of bread and meat and Adriel's lips twitched, though he didn't say anything else. I ate the rest of my sandwich, even though I wasn't really hungry, getting the sense that Adriel would not be satisfied until I had eaten every last bite.

When I had eaten the sandwich, I smiled as I reached for the mug of tea that was proper Irish tea. Molly had been true to her word that she would stock the kitchen with it. I added some milk after taking out the teabag and added a spoon of sugar to help in case I went into delayed shock. Adriel took the tray from me and set it at the end of the bed before returning to his original position.

"Kalila said that the kitchen mistress asked her to put the tea in the League kitchen for you, that you would prefer it to the weak tea that the angels liked. She made the sandwich herself. The poor angel looked quite stricken when Nathaniel carried you up here."

I took a sip of my tea, then held the mug in my hand. "Has she ever tried to make you feel...less...?"

My words trailed off because I didn't exactly know how Adriel felt deep down because he had perfected the art of appearing like nothing mattered at all, that he no longer felt anything. It was only when he slipped, when the mask fell, that I saw the real Adriel.

"I was feral when Nathaniel and the League rescued me. I couldn't differentiate friend from foe. I didn't recognise my own twin. When I saw Adair, I thought it was my mind taunting me with the perfect face that had once been mine." His tone is even, like he is recalling a story but not truly remembering the feelings in that moment. I knew what that was like. It would be how I remembered what had happened in the courtyard today.

"I was confined to a room and I think it was the fifth day, Nathaniel brought Kalila in and she tried to take away my pain to clear my head. I snapped. I let all of the emotions in me spill out so someone would understand. I could have killed her. She never looked at me the same again. Not that I blame her. She saw the monster I had become deep inside."

I nudged him with my shoulder. "I don't think that Kalila has it in her to think bad of anyone."

"You did not hear her when she realized what Abraxas had done, what he meant to do. I think if she could have taken the knife she was using to cut off a certain appendage, she might have done so."

"Damn, I'd have paid to see that." I let loose a chuckle, turning the warm mug in my hands. "What will happen to Abraxas now?"

Adriel didn't answer me and I set my mug down on the side table and made to get out of bed.

"Where are you going?" Adriel asked, having not moved an inch from the bed.

"To see what's happening since you are not going to tell me. And I would have thought that you'd want to be there if he was being punished."

Looking at Adriel, I watched as his lips curved into a bitter smirk. "I am the bogeyman the angels fear. I do not have to be there as they punish him, the threat of me will be enough to scare him. Verena knows that he is afraid of me, as he should be, and she will do her thing. The threat of me is enough that my presence isn't required."

I see the coldness in his eyes as Adriel looked at me, his eyes bleeding to pure obsidian for a split second. "Besides, I would just kill him and his penance would be done. He'd suffer first of course, but a dead angel can feel no pain."

With a sigh I climbed back into the bed and picked up my mug again. I took a long sip to see of it would heat the blood in my veins and stayed quiet after Adriel's statement.

"Have I frightened you now?" He asked me, and I turned in the bed so I could look at him.

"Hell no. You might not believe me but I would tell you if I was afraid of you." Adriel seemed sceptical, so I elaborated. "Could you kill me if you had just cause? Absolfuckinglutely. I would do the same. If you let loose the darkness and I had to hurt you to help you, then I would. I would do it because I know that you would not want innocent people hurt. Hurting you in the moment helps you in the end."

Adriel looked at me, his expression blank and then he smiled. "Yes, I do think if I lost control, it would be you who would be the first to react. I would be glad of it. How is it that you have such a military mind?"

Shrugging, I drained my tea and set the mug down, then pulled the blankets up higher. "I started sitting in on strategy meetings with my mother when I was three or four. I used to sneak around the camp and listen in during military drills and that. I didn't understand exactly what it all meant, but I just committed it to memory. It served me well when I was training and then when I was sent on my first proper mission."

"How old were you?"

"Seven," I replied, running a hand though my hair. "There was this bunker that a scouting team had found that had food and supplies. The only way in was a small window because the door had been welded shut. I was the smallest so I went in to look for another way in. One of the people in the bunker was still alive, had eaten her family to stay alive. I had to kill her."

"So young."

"We were at war. We still are. I suppose it won't make you feel any better if I tell you that wasn't even my first kill. That was a few months earlier."

Adriel's hands clenched in his lap; however, he didn't respond to that admission. It felt good to be able to tell my secrets to someone who didn't judge me. Maybe Adriel could understand that I was a victim of circumstances, though I hated to think of myself as a victim.

"Keep struggling. I like it."

Abraxas' voice inside my head made me shudder, and I gripped the sheets tighter.

"It was to prepare us in the event we had to kill. So, we wouldn't be shocked when we had to do it. The leaders and our older soldiers would bring prisoners of war into a locked room and we had to kill to survive. Beforehand they told us of the crimes the person had committed. They put me in a room with a man who had a liking for dark-haired little girls."

Adriel was quiet for a couple of minutes before he said. "It sounds like the training we had with the League. As a healer, it went against our very nature to kill someone, even in defence. Our power wanted to heal them even as they lay dying. But it was necessary for us to not be a liability on the battlefield."

"Is that why Adair was so upset when I tossed at him that he was as bad as Abraxas and Rieka when he healed me so they could break my bones again?"

Adriel nodded. "Adair could never compartmentalize it like I could. He always looked on the brighter side of life. I did too, once. I remember how it used to feel."

This conversation was getting very dark and very heavy.

"We've been through so much in our very long lives." I mused, trying to be funny, and it worked making Adriel laugh.

"I have centuries on you, Raven. I am allowed to be more cynical than you."

"Yano, it's strange to think that I'll be twenty-one in a few weeks and that feels so young and old at the same time." I admitted, almost forgetting that my birthday would be happening soon. When I was locked up in the dungeons, I'd only made note of the date in order to try and remember the number of days that had passed since my foiled assassination attempt.

"Angels don't celebrate birthdays." Adriel said, running a hand through his hair. "We live for eons so celebrating the day we were born seems frivolous. But I know that some humans make a big deal out of some birthdays. Is twenty-one considered a big deal?"

"Yup. If I was at home, we'd be planning a big fuck off party. The boys would probably get me drunk so that I'd be dying the next morning with the mother of all hangovers. There would be music, and presents, and a cake for me to make a wish on."

"And what would you wish for, Raven, if you could wish for anything?"

Closing my eyes, I considered his question. "To go home. To go back home." A dark whisper crept into my mind and before I could stop myself, I found myself saying. "No, if I'm being honest, I don't even think that I would wish to go home. I'd wish to know what it was like to fly. To have wings. To have the freedom to take to the skies and see the world from above. It's what I used to wish for when I was a child. Though I never told a soul about it."

"There is only one angel who can grant you that wish but I think you would rather bleed than ask it of him."

I shook my head vigorously. "No. I'd never ask him. It would feel like he had one over on me then and I'd hate the thought of owing him. Unless you fancy playing the big scary angel and just taking me for a spin?"

Wiggling my eyebrows, I grinned and Adriel chuckled softly. "Know that I would, if I could. With the way you keep trying to flirt with your mortality, I fear it is best to not do anything that pisses Nathaniel off enough that I am not around to keep the grim reaper from your door."

"Tell the truth, your life would be so fucking boring without me around."

Adriel shook his head but he was smiling. I couldn't stop myself from wondering what was happening to Abraxas. I hoped he was suffering. I wanted him to suffer. And part of me wanted to see him suffer.

"Nathaniel will disable his wings. That will keep him landbound until the feathers grow back. He will be ordered to stay away from anywhere you might venture. He will be ostracized from the League and any and all members of the League will be ordered to give Abraxas a wide berth. That includes Saskia, though even Sparkles won't want to entertain an angel who tried to take a woman by force."

"If he tried that in the human world, someone would have killed him."

"The number of soldiers has diminished and the League needs all of its soldiers for when Ascian brings the fight to our door. The Imperium would not allow Nathaniel to kill him when his power is a valuable asset against the Seraphan."

I didn't like it...I didn't like it one bit.

"Next time he tries anything, I'll kill him, Adriel. I won't let him get close enough to touch me like that again. I don't care about his powers or the war with the Seraphan. I'll kill him to save my own life."

"I know."

That was all that Adriel said in response, and we lapsed into a comfortable silence. I closed my eyes and leaned my head against the pillow, listening to the faint sound of Grainger's rumbled snoring and the sound of my own heartbeat.

The sudden panic that I had shoved down after Abraxas' attack bubbled to the surface and I couldn't breathe, I couldn't think, I felt like I was dying.

"Did you know that it was possible for an angel to break a human's pelvis with one hard thrust?"

I can hear the bastard's voice in my head, I can feel his hands on my body and I instantly feel dirty again. I'd brought this on me myself. I had taunted him, berated him, and goaded him into seeking retribution for making a fool of him. Abraxas was a predator and I had made myself prey to him.

"Keep struggling. I like it."

"Raven."

Adriel's voice dragged me from the replay of events going on in my head. I exhaled some air, then, held my hands out, watched as they trembled, forced them to steady. I blinked my eyes a few times, then ground my teeth together.

"I fucking goaded him into attacking me. I went looking for trouble and my fucking hubris almost got the better of me. I hate feeling like a victim, Adriel."

"Would you think me a victim for that which

happened to me?" Adriel asked me, his shoulder pressed against mine, as if it was the only way he could offer me comfort.

"No." I said, before I reiterated it. "Hell no. You survived when most wouldn't. You kept going when there was no hope. That doesn't make you a victim, Adriel, it makes you a survivor."

"Zadkiel used to tell me that you should never trust a survivor, not until you find out what he did in order to stay alive."

"Then Zadkiel was a fool who didn't understand that the world wasn't black and white, there are shades of grey and situations that don't follow any training procedure drilled into us. War is bloody, war is fucking brutal. We do what we have to in order to survive and fuck anyone who criticizes us for it."

I feel the weight of understanding in his eyes as Adriel looked over at the window. I yawned, tiredness wanting to yank me into sleep, though I knew if I slept, I would probably have nightmares and I'd embarrassed myself enough today, didn't want to add more shame to the list of shit I'd done wrong today.

"Your trauma has made you stronger." Adriel said, glancing at me but I was already shaking my head.

"No. Don't give it that kind of power over me. Over you." I replied to Adriel, hugging my knees to my chest. "My trauma made me traumatised. It weakened me. It's affected my ability to trust, and messed with my emotions. I relive my traumas when I'm asleep and when I'm awake, at the most inconvenient times. I made myself stronger every single time I succeeded in dragging myself out of the darkness and dealt with consequences that were never my fault. The traumas we inherited were just part of the shitty hand we were dealt."

"That is a strangely healthy way of looking at it."

I barked out a laugh. "Like fuck it is. Do you think I believe half the shit I say? I mean, most of it is to make sure that I don't let it all out at the same time and either become a blubbering mess or a homicidal maniac. Though, considering how many times I've been close to death since I tried to kill the Imperium, some might say I was indeed flirting with death instead of playing hard to get."

"Perhaps we should try and put pause on this liking for danger and death for a time. You'll make me old and grey with worry."

"I can't make any promises. I do not have control of my life. Shit happens." I laughed, laying my head down on the pillow, and closed my eyes.

Images started to whirl through my mind and I tossed onto my side, grinding my teeth together. A hand fell on my shoulder and I opened my eyes to look into dark green eyes. "Sleep, Raven. No nightmares will dare to haunt you this night, not when the real nightmare is already right next to you."

I found that strangely comforting and while I didn't say that to Adriel, I did snuggle down further under the covers. Letting my eyes drift shut, the hand on my shoulder felt like I was being anchored to the present and not held captive by the past. For once, it was nice to think that there was a bigger, badder monster watching over me. I should have been terrified of Adriel's hand on me but I wasn't because I was used to sharing a bed with a monster.

But the monster in the dark was always me...

T he next couple of days passed by without much incident. Adriel had been beside me when I woke the day after Abraxas, and had ordered me not to train for that day and the next. Instead, I was kept busy by invites to hang out with Dev and V, and watched the angels spar after demanding that they let me out into the courtyard since I guessed that they were keeping me away from the place me and Abraxas had fought in case I ended up with PTSD or some shit.

Nathaniel had eventually told me that Abraxas had told Adriel that Nathaniel had requested his presence on the perimeter, and once Adriel had flown out, they had both realized that Abraxas had meant to isolate me. As fast as they could, they'd both flown back just in time to stop Abraxas from raping me.

When I'd said it out loud, the angels had flinched, but denying it wouldn't get us anywhere.

The other elephant in the room was the kiss we had

shared. Nathaniel hadn't mentioned it and neither had I, yet it hung in the air like an attacker waiting to pounce. Despite everything else going on I couldn't let myself wonder what it would be like for Nathaniel to kiss me without restraint. I literally couldn't stop thinking about it. It was becoming very inconvenient, and it was really starting to do my head in.

Even now as Nathaniel sat across the way from me as we played chess, I tried to focus on the game but my eyes kept landing on his lips. When everyone had retired for the night, me and Nathaniel had stayed to finish our game, leaving us alone in the room. Right now, the arrogant SOB was sitting back in his chair, a smug smile on his face because we both knew he'd have checkmate in one move.

"Stop looking so fucking smug. You do realize that you've had God knows how many years playing this game and I'm a newbie. Six more months and I'll kick your ass."

Nathaniel chuckled, folding his arms across his chest. "We did not have chess back home. It was something Adriel studied in order to focus his mind after he returned to us. We learned to play so he could have someone to play against. So contrary to what you believe, we only have a handful of years of knowledge. Though the speed in which you have picked it up is tremendous."

My cheeks heated a little at the praise in his tone and I ducked my head to focus on the board. "It's like a military strategy. It's like the pieces on the board are your army and you have to move them in order not to concede defeat. Maybe that's why my mind likes it. Though I hate losing and even I can see that you've won. But I can't just hand you the win. I can't go easy on you. I don't have that in me."

"Perish the thought that Raven Cassidy would ever go easy on me."

Rolling my eyes, I sighed, and then growled, holding out my hand to concede victory to Nathaniel. His hand gripped mine, his hand warm in mine, and my heart kicked up into a gallop.

"Raven..." Nathaniel started, but the door to the study flung open and Cassiopeia rushed in, her face grim. Cassiopeia was an angel who could command you to do anything with a spoken command. She didn't like me very much and I think if she could command me to walk into the pointed end of a blade, she would. Then again, I had thrown an axe at her in my attempt to escape after Aramis so that might be the reason why she hated me. Her gaze slid from me to Nathaniel, before a muscle ticked in her jaw, her blue back wings shifting slightly.

Dropping my hand, Nathaniel was on his feet. "What is it Cass?"

"There has been an incident. The Imperium has recalled all the League and requests your presence in the throne room."

Nathaniel glanced at me. "I'll see you later."

"The Imperium has requested that Raven attend also. I was sent to make sure that you both comply."

Nathaniel glared at Cassiopeia and it looked like he might argue with her. I got to my feet and touched his elbow. "It's grand. Let's get this over with."

I strode out passed Cassiopeia and headed down toward the throne room. Mentally preparing myself for whatever horrors Rieka was now going to force me to watch, I was aware of the chilled silence behind me, like the angels were aware that this was not going to be anything warm and fuzzy. It wasn't like the bitch was gonna set me free or anything. She probably just wanted to remind me that she was in charge and the reason I hadn't seen her in months was because she had made it so.

Nathaniel called my name as I rounded the corner and had a hand on the door, but I didn't wait, I just shoved open the doors and walked in. Cassiopeia had not been exaggerating when she said that the entire League of Dominious was here. The only one that seemed to be missing was Abraxas, and to be honest, I was glad for that.

The League was standing in a relaxed stance, the same grim expression as Cassiopeia on their faces. They all looked straight ahead, but Adriel broke rank to glance at me, his eyes warning me without him having to say a word. My heart started to beat a little faster and I stood on the fringes as Cassiopeia fell into line beside the League.

I ran my gaze down the line, starting with Saskia, then Asterin, Draegan, Adair, Adriel, Devika, Makata, and Verena. The only other angel in the room was Hannele, which was surprising as she stood close to the Imperium. Nathaniel brushed his hand against the small of my back and then went to the dais where his mother and Imperium of the angels reclined in her chair.

Rieka had wings of molten gold, with yellow eyes, and hair that was a lighter shade of a sandy blonde. She wore a white ensemble; a white pair of pants that clung to the muscles in her legs, and her heels looked like they were a weapon in themselves. The jacket she wore was long sleeve, the front in a blazer style and then it swept down into a long cloak that would no doubt trail after her as she sauntered around the citadel. A lace insert covered her breasts, but came down in a vee to show off her cleavage. It was like she liked to give those who would admire her a little taste of what they would never have. A belt at her waist held the jacket in place and the buckle had a wing carved into it.

Her beautiful face held the arrogance of a leader who ruled through blood and fear, and the only thing that separated her from Abraxas, was that Rieka actually had power. Not a physical power, no. Her power was to leech the active powers of other angels and use them tenfold. I was lucky that she couldn't use mine, or Adriel's because if she had been able to use his, then there is no doubt that all the Rebels would be dead.

"Why is there a human girl bound and gagged on the ground?" Nathaniel asked and it snapped me from my thoughts and I concentrated on the human on her knees in front of the Imperium.

She looked maybe a year or two younger than me,

with mousy brown hair and a shockingly thin face. Her body was thin, almost malnourished and I knew she had lived in one of the farther away communities that had suffered the most due to lack of food and supplies. Her eyes were big and blue, and she was shaking, like she knew her death was coming.

Rieka kept her yellow eyes trained on me as she waved a hand in the air. "The human has been detained for murder. She snuck into the citadel somehow, went to the home of an angel and used some sort of contraption to bolt her wings to the wall, and then shot one of those bolts into her heart. By the time Adair was summoned, Farren was already dead."

Nathaniel glanced down at the girl, and she shrunk into herself. "How could that tiny girl have taken down an angel with just a weapon?"

"Farren was with a bedfellow who outlined what had happened. Apparently, Farren was on top and her wings were outstretched and the girl came out of the wardrobe and shot her whilst she was in the throes of passion."

Laughter bubbled in my chest and it slipped out before I had the good sense to stop it. "Well, at least she died happy. Gives new meaning to little death, right?"

Rieka pointed a finger at me. "You will hold your tongue or I will have Cassiopeia make it so."

That made me chuckle again. "Then where would the fun be in that, Rieka? I mean, you summoned me here to witness whatever you have planned, right? So, you had to anticipate that I'd hardly stand here and do what you tell me. I think you like this back and forth between us.

It's probably been a long time since someone has called you out on your bullshit."

I could see the unbridled rage in Rieka's eyes as she slid her gaze to her son. "Nathaniel, muzzle your pet or I will do it for you."

Nathaniel didn't even glance in my direction as I came to stand beside the girl, who looked up at me, her eyes widening and I offered her a small smile. There was no hope in her eyes, like she knew death was coming for her and I knew that look; I'd worn the same look over three years ago when I had come to kill the Imperium.

"Has anyone even bothered to ask the girl why she killed this Farran? Or have you just judged her because she's human?"

"There is no justification for the murder of an angel." Rieka remarked blandly, and I felt the rage simmer inside me, wanting to get out.

"Of course not. But if you are gonna condemn her to death, then the fucking least thing you owe her is to hear her story."

Without waiting for permission, I gave Rieka my back and crouched down in front of the girl. I pulled down her gag, and she coughed. I asked for a bottle of water, making sure that Nathaniel took a sip before I did, and then I held it to the girl's lips for her to drink.

"An taibhse." The girl said, making me smile. Her accent was definitely southern Ireland, thicker than my Cork accent so more Kerry if I heard right.

"The ghost? Is that what they are calling me now? The others get cool nicknames and I get called a ghost?"

"Is it you?"

I pulled my power around me for a second before I let it go again. "What's your name?"

"Noelle."

I offered her a small smile. "I'm Raven."

"I know who you are. We all know who you are." The girl said, the admiration in her voice like I was some sort of celebrity or something.

"You wanna tell me what happened?"

"An bhfuil Gaeilge agat?" Noelle asked me, and I glanced back at Hannele, knowing that she was already translating the Irish into its English meaning, do you speak Irish?

"Tá," Yes, I told her when I looked back at her, then advised her that so could one of the angels. "Ach mar sin is féidir le duine de na haingil."

Noelle looked crestfallen, but I reached out and touched her shoulder. "It's grand. My Irish is probably rusty from not using it. English is fine, Noelle. Tell me what happened."

Noelle swallowed hard, then blew out a breath. "My brother, Mathew, he worked on the farmland just outside the citadel. Our parents were farmers before... and Mathew tended our farm as long as possible after they died. An angel saw him and brought him here to tend the farm. He told me that an angel had taken interest in him and maybe it might get us some more food."

Nodding my head, encouraging her to continue, the girl did. "Mathew vanished a few days later and they found his body twisted and broken near the wastelands. He'd been... used, bones broken and shattered in places that seemed impossible. I heard that this Farran had broken his pelvis and thrown my big brother out like he was nothing but rubbish."

"Did you know that it was possible for an angel to break a human's pelvis with one hard thrust?"

I heard the flames of anger in her tone as I tried to ignore Abraxas' voice in my head, and I echoed them when I said. "Did she suffer when you killed her?"

"I think so."

"Good. How'd you do it?"

"It was the bolt gun we used on the farm to kill the cattle. It worked on birds so I said I would try it on the angel. The ones in her wings kept her immobile while I shot the last bolt into her heart."

Glancing over my shoulder at Rieka, I flashed her a feral grin. "I might need to invest in one of those."

Turning back to Noelle, I asked her to describe the angel who she had killed, and to be fair, I wasn't too surprised when I heard the description. Looking up at Nathaniel, I lifted my brows. "Farren is the angel who talked about humans being breakable with Akora. Looks like the two of them were in on it together."

"Enough of this." Rieka said, waving her hand in the air. "The human must die. She murdered one of my angels and her punishment is set."

"You should be rewarding her for taking out the trash, not killing her. Unless you were aware that your angels were raping and murdering humans and did fuck all about it? Then that makes you an even bigger bitch than I already knew you were."

"Raven." Nathaniel's tone wasn't exactly chastising, more a warning but I ignored him, keeping my focus on the Imperium.

Rieka's lips curved into a smile that had my stomach sinking, and I could almost feel the dread that came with a smile like that. The Imperium shifted her gaze from mine, then along the League of Dominious, and I could have almost predicted her next move before she made it.

"Adriel. Kill the human."

It would seem that Rieka played chess very well.

"No." My friend ground out, his open act of defiance treason in his angelic world.

"You will do as your Imperium orders of you. I can see it in your eyes, Adriel. I can see how much your power craves her death. Lay your hands upon her and make her scream for me. Punish her for the act of murder against your kin. Feed that power of yours."

Adriel's eyes had gone from their dark green to black, his fists clenched at his sides as Noelle shivered in front of me. Even from over here, I could tell that Adriel was close to losing control, the temptation of death almost too much for him to reign in. Black veins spread out from his eyes, like I had seen before, but this time, they also travelled down his arms, like the death power was already going to his hands for him to use.

"Now, Adriel. Or I will call Abraxas and let him have some time with her. It might cheer him up to take out some of his...aggression... on the girl."

"You have no idea just how badly I want to put your head through the wall." I snarled at Rieka, who smirked at me, even as Adriel stepped forward, his movements jerky.

Noelle grabbed my leg, and even I could smell the fear coming off her. Adriel took another step towards us and I blocked Noelle from view, hoping that Adriel would snap out of it and see me. But he had this hungry expression on his face and it made my heart ache.

I couldn't let Adriel lose himself to the power in him. He would never forgive himself for the pain he would no doubt inflict on the girl, a human was far less durable than an angel. He'd retreat into himself and lose another part of him. I couldn't and wouldn't allow that to happen.

Adriel stood in front of me, his head slightly tilted, the back inky streaks pulsing on his tanned skin. "Move, Raven."

I braced my hands on my hips. "Go fuck yourself, Adriel. You want her, you gotta go through me."

"I could kill you."

I shrugged, flashing him a toothy grin. "You were the one who told me that I liked to flirt with death."

There was a flash of green in his eyes and I knew my friend was still in there. He didn't want to do this...and he didn't have to.

Glancing over at the Imperium, I realized that Rieka was playing a game with us, amusing herself. She wanted to break the bonds I had with the angels. This was revenge for Abraxas. And in that moment, I knew she had never intended for Adriel to kill Noelle.

This was a play of power. A display of authority. Rieka didn't even have to lift a manicured finger and chaos was raging all around her, like she was a puppet master. I hated her so venomously in that moment, knowing I had been manipulated and I hated myself for it too.

"You've made your fucking point, Rieka. You've made your fucking point." I looked away from her before I could see the triumph in her yellow eyes, locking gazes with Adriel as I said. "I'll kill her. I'll be the one to fucking kill her."

A driel snarled as I said it, though I wasn't sure if it was in relief or because he wasn't going to be the one who was the hand of death this night. However, Adriel stepped back, closing his eyes and when he opened them, his eyes had returned to green. The black veins pulsed before fading, and he was Adriel once more.

"Raven...I..." His voice trailed off as I walked over to him and grabbed his arm.

"It's okay, my friend. I'll make it quick, and painless. Neither you nor her should suffer because that bitch wants to put me in my place."

Releasing his arm, I turned back to Noelle. I sat down on the ground in front of her and removed the bindings on her wrists. Her hands shook and I took them in mine, forcing her to still and look at me.

"I'm glad it will be you." Noelle said, her voice trembling. "The captain told me that you would be merciful and kind if I met you."

The captain. Tiernan. Tiernan had sent her to me knowing that I was the only one who could grant her a merciful death. He was called the captain because he was the captain of our little group and trained us with the efficiency needed to be the best at what we did.

"And he knows me better than anyone, does the captain. He has the dreamiest eyes I've ever seen in my life too. Makes all the girls and boys swoon." Noelle laughed as her cheeks pinkened and I ignored everyone else around us. "Not me though. But if he told you that I will be merciful then believe him, I always have."

Noelle reached for something under the collar of her shirt, a silver cross that glinted in the candlelight. "Are you religious?"

I was about to snort, but I didn't have it in me to mock her faith even in the darkest of these days. "No. Not in the slightest. I learned like everyone else but it never stuck."

"My mam used to say in the early days that the angels were sent from God. This was her cross. I remember a quote she used to say all the damn time; Are not all angels ministering spirits sent to serve those who will inherit salvation? She still believed that even up to when my parents were killed for attending church on Sunday."

Squeezing her hands, I said. "We had a priest in our camp during the first few years until he witnessed too much horror and we had to kill him. He rambled and rambled about scripture, and this one quote stuck with me. And the angels who did not keep their positions of authority but abandoned their proper dwelling—these he has kept in darkness, bound with everlasting chains for judgment on the great Day."

I ignored the sharp intake of breath to the side, knowing the passage from the bible would strike a chord with the angels. Ascian had bound this world in darkness and the quote likened him to God. It seemed appropriate, considering that Ascian also had the means of reopening the door in the angel Niran, the invisible chains of this hold on those not Seraphan a metaphor in itself.

"Will it hurt? Dying?"

"I'll make it quick. Painless."

Noelle closed her eyes, taking her hands from mine and holding them together before I heard her say. "Ár nAthair, atá ar neamh,"

She was praying the Our Father in Irish and I listened to her, trying to keep my own emotions at bay. I needed to stay calm, I needed to not show her that my heart was breaking at the fact that her death was another one to add to my tally. I didn't want Adriel to see just how much it took from me to do this so he wouldn't have to.

"I can do it, Raven."

I peered up at Nathaniel, shaking my head. "That would defeat the purpose. This whole production was for me. To put me back in my place. There was never going to be any other outcome, Nathaniel. I would either have to kill her or watch Adriel do it and maybe have it destroy him. Your bitch of a mother knew I'd offer to do it to save him. If I don't do it now, she'll find someone else to use against me."

Nathaniel looked like he didn't like my assessment all that much, but he gave a slight incline of his head, leaving me to focus on Noelle. Her eyes watched me with this reverence that I didn't deserve.

"I always wanted to be a soldier. I really did, but Mathew said that the Rebels needed skilled workers to provide them with milk and meat in order to fight the angels."

I reached out and cupped her cheek. "Tonight, you became a soldier, Noelle. You are as much a Rebel as I am. It's in your veins. I will tell them about your bravery. I will tell them of your courage when I get the chance. I will tell the Rebels about Mathew and about you. Mo chara, my friend, I will not let you or Mathew be forgotten."

A single tear slipped down her cheek and I wiped it away. "No. No tears now. They don't deserve your tears. They don't get to see that."

Noelle blinked away her tears, and I was proud of her backbone of steel. "Will you sing the national anthem with me?"

I offered her a small laugh. "Jesus, if I start singing, you might start crying again."

"Please, Raven. Let me die as you said, like a soldier."

If that was her dying wish, then I had to grant it. "Close your eyes, Noelle. Mathew is waiting for you on the other side."

Noelle closed her eyes as I got to my feet and she started to sing the lyrics to Amhrán na bhFiann, The Soldier's Song. Forcing a mask to slide over my features, I walked to stand behind Noelle, my voice joining in with hers as we sang it in English, so the fucking angels would know exactly what we sang.

> "Soldiers are we,
>
> Whose lives are pledged to Ireland,
>
> Some have come from a land beyond the wave,
>
> Sworn to be free, no more our ancient Ireland
>
> Shall shelter the despot or the slave;
>
> Tonight we man the Bearna Baoil
>
> In Erin's cause come woe or weal,"

While we sang, I used my right hand to cup Noelle on the face, her words wavering as I touched her. Then I used my left hand to brace on her shoulder so that I could use that to steady my grip. I waited until we were near the end of the song, lifting my gaze to Rieka defiantly as we sang.

> "'Mid cannon's roar and rifle's peal,
>
> We'll chant a soldier's song."

The moment we sang the word song, I twisted hard, with enough force to snap Noelle's neck with an audible crack. Her body sagged in my grasp, my stomach lurching and I swallowed down the bile in my throat.

Lowering Noelle to the ground, I lay down gently, then reached over to make sure her eyes were still closed. Sliding my hand down to her chest, I held it to her chest, just over her heart. "May the souls of all the faithful departed, through the mercy of God, rest in peace. Amen."

"Are you done with your performance yet?"

My head snapped up. Rieka held up a hand to stop Nathaniel from putting himself between us. Rising to my feet, I glared at Rieka, my anger hot and furiously burning inside me. "Go fuck yourself, Rieka."

"Your crudeness isn't appealing, Raven. It just proves how common and unremarkable you are. Now that you have seen that I do not have to even spill a drop of blood to wield my control over you. My son might think that you are his little creature, but I hold your leash, Raven. Do not forget that."

I wanted to punch the bitch. I wanted to grab a knife and slit her fucking throat. She thought she knew who I was, what I was. But Noelle had helped me remember. She reminded me that I was a Rebel, that I was a weapon forged in darkness and drenched in blood. She would not break me...more formidable monsters had tried to do so and fucking failed.

Clapping my hands in a sarcastic slow gesture, I walked around Noelle's body, putting myself within a short striking distance of the Imperium. I still had a Nathaniel sized barrier in my path to her. But I wouldn't take a shot today...no...Rieka's expression told me she had bated me with that intention so that she could have a reason to use one of the angels against me.

"Well done. Well fucking done." I started as I continued to clap. "You outsmarted me. I hope you are pleased with yourself because it won't happen again. Fool me once and all that bullshit."

"It was never about outsmarting you, Raven. It was about making sure you knew your place."

"The thing is Rieka, I always knew my place. It was just different from the place that you have allotted me in your twisted brain."

Rieka curved her lips into a smug smile, like she thought herself to be winning and her attempts to poke at me had succeeded. I had to show her that her actions hadn't struck me as hard as she might have wanted.

"You know what the problem is with people like you, Rieka? Once you have tasted power, it consumes you. You'll do whatever the fuck you can to try and keep a firm grip on it. You hide it well, the fear of losing it, but I see you. I've seen people just like you. Hell, I was raised by people just like you. Ruthless, focused, and so certain of their power that they can't even dream that someone else might take them down a peg or two."

I paused as I drew in a breath, continuing on before Rieka had a chance to interject. "Leaders like you, those who cling to power by sending others to fight for them? They will never truly understand why it is we fight. But I'm just a soldier. That's always been my path, ever since I was handed a gun at five years old. Ever since I was taught how to take pain without uttering a sound. I was just another weapon to be welded and a bloody good one at that."

I'm not sure who, but one of the angels behind me sucked in a breath as if they can't believe anyone who make a weapon out of a child. But there was no time for us to be children in a world where angels rule with an iron fist. We were forged in fire in a world where no one expected an angel to set the world alight.

"Your crown isn't guaranteed. You use those around you to stay on your gilded throne when in reality, any one of the League could fight you for the Imperium title and win. The very angel you wanted to exploit to get at me could reign over this country, and never have to lift his hand because his power is greater than yours, and even you know it. If you keep treating those who support you like animals who are at your beck and call and soon, they might just bite back."

Rieka is looking at me, studying me and her eyes don't even flicker as I speak, like she can't comprehend that one day, an angel would dare rise up against her. She rests her chin on her hand, waving the other one at me. "Are you quite finished?"

"Your hubris will be your downfall. Your arrogance will be your undoing. And I will laugh my ass off when it happens. But if there is a God, I'll be the one to give you exactly what you deserve."

Not waiting for her to continue, I turn around and gather Noelle in my arms, not sparing a glance at the angels as I made to carry her from the room.

"I have not dismissed you." Rieka's voice boomed like thunder and I wished that I could balance Noelle's body well enough to flip her off and show her just how crude I could be.

"You are more than fucking welcome to try and stop me, Rieka. More than fucking welcome."

I kept on walking, straight down the hall and headed toward the human quarters. Angels and humans alike got out of my way as I carried Noelle, my heart starting to beat faster and faster as the calm façade started to shatter inside me. My legs trembled and I knew I wouldn't be able to carry Noelle down the compact stairs easily.

There was a human boy coming up the stairs as I came closer, and his eyes bulged when he saw me carrying the dead body. "Get me Michael and Molly." I snarled and then the boy rushed down the stairs.

Leaning against the wall for support, my arms aching but I refused to let her down. Hayes appeared up the stairs, his eyes wide as he came over and took some of the weight from me.

"What the hell happened?"

I shook my head, unable to get passed the emotion that was thick in my throat. It was too raw, too fresh to explain to Hayes in an unfeeling way. "I can't. Her name is Noelle. She was a farmer's daughter." I explained as Molly came up the stairs and looked at the slain girl, her expression grim and her eyes sad.

"I didn't want the angels to bury her. She died a soldier. She needs a soldier's funeral. Promise me, Hayes. Promise me that you'll look after her."

"She's one of us, Raven. I'll make sure she gets the funeral she deserves. You can give her to me, now."

I handed her over to Hayes, who waited for a second,

this torn look on his face until Molly came forward. "Go boy. Raven will be grand."

The moment Hayes disappeared down the stairs with Noelle, I slid down the wall and screamed until my throat felt raw. Then I bolted upright, ignoring Molly's face as I headed back down the corridor.

"Raven."

I halted, glancing over my shoulder at the older woman. "You did well by her."

I barked out a laugh. "I killed her. I snapped her neck."

"But you did it cleanly. With compassion. And it's better than she would have gotten from the angels."

That didn't assuage my guilt in the slightest.

I trudged back to the League quarters, wanting to lock myself away in my room and allow myself to grieve for the girl who didn't have to die. To mourn the loss of another human life to the angel's tyranny. She deserved to have someone feel sorry that she was dead, even if it was the person who had taken her life.

Climbing the steps, I got to the top and stopped at seeing an angel waiting for me, and out of all the angels, it was a surprise to see Adair standing there. His face was pinched tight, his bright green eyes sombre as he lifted his head to look at me. I didn't want a confrontation. I didn't want him to have a go at me when I was on the verge of breaking down.

"Adair..."

The angel strode forward and embraced me, holding me tight against his chest, leaving me with no option but to wrap my arm around his back, my fingers grazing his wings.

"Thank you," Adair murmured into my ear. "Thank you for protecting him. For saving him. Ever since you came into his life, parts of my twin have come back and if he had been forced to kill her, I don't think he could come back from the dark again."

Adair let me go and I stood there, broken and battered on the inside. I would take a beating any day of the week over the gut-wrenching emotions Noelle's death had stirred in me. I didn't want or need Adair's thanks, though I knew why he felt he needed to come and offer it to me. We hadn't exactly started out on the best of terms, with him healing my injuries when I was tortured, him decking me for thinking I was toying with Adriel, to now thanking me for the care and consideration I had shown his brother.

Emotion had a vice grip around my throat, my head pounding as I touched my hand to Adair's, then left him standing in the hallway. I closed the door behind me, and went into the bathroom, and vomited the contents of my stomach into the sink. When that was over, I threw some water on my face, hoping the cold would shock me out of the tirade of sadness and guilt that was threatening to bury me under its avalanche.

My eyes were blurry with tears, and I tried to stuff them down. One rebellious tear slid down my cheek and it unlocked the dam inside me, the tears now flowing freely. A sob escaped my lips as I swept my hand out and sent all the things on the shelf over the sink flying.

I walked over to the wall and slid down it, pouring out all of my pain, all of my sorrow, not just from tonight, but from my entire fucking life. My chest ached, my heart ached, and I hated feeling so terribly human. Resting my face in my hands, I let loose another scream, my voice cracking as my tears ran dry and I just sat there, in the bathroom, in the dark, and let the silence and darkness wrap around me like a comforting blanket.

It was, after all, where I truly belonged.

I was unsure of how long I sat in the darkness, but it seemed like a considerable amount of time. The numbness had taken root in my bones and I had not felt this unravelled in a long, long time. Since they put a gun or a weapon in my hand as a child, most of my killings were of wastelanders, of traitors, and of course an angel or two, but that wasn't something I was going to brag to the angels about.

But the winter I turned twelve, we lost an entire squad to the angels. They were massacred the moment they stepped out of the coverage of the safehouse. Someone must have leaked their location to the angels and played a hand in their slaughter. The soldiers had been on a medicine run, picking up packages left at the safehouse by doctors and chemists, who worked close enough to the citadel to get their hands on ingredients to make salves and pain relief.

Two months of supplies were destroyed in the ambush.

The leaders had spent weeks trying to sniff out the mole and, in the end, later one night while I was sneaking around the barracks, I overheard a conversation that led us to the traitor right under our own roof.

The guilty party had been talking to one of the soldiers, a man who was known to run a gambling racket with the other soldiers and they were arguing, with the lying piece of shit telling his bookie that he'd have the rest of the coin next week.

Money was a useless commodity to us humans. We bartered with food and skills, with the angels being the ones that traded in coin. They forged it within the walls of their citadel, and the Elites, the rich humans who sold out their own kind to bask in the wealth and opulence of the angels, were the ones who coveted the currency. The only Rebels who had access to the angel's coin were the ones who worked in the marketplace and those who conspired with angels.

When I realized that this soldier must have been the one who sold out his own soldiers in order to pay a gambling debt, I marched straight to my mother and told her. It had made me a little uneasy when I had seen the pride in her eyes, like she had to keep searching for proof that I was not secretly aligned with the angels because I happened to have their blood in my veins.

Though I never expected them to want me to give them a display of my loyalty, even at twelve years old.

Tiernan had come and called me out of my room in the

barracks and told me to follow him. I hurried after him eagerly, because Tiernan was older than me, already a soldier in every sense and I would follow him anywhere. He didn't speak as we left the sleeping quarters and headed down to the interrogation rooms.

My stomach flipped when we went down the stone steps and I could hear screams in the distance. I ground to a halt, wondering what I had down to deserve this after I had been the one to find the man who had betrayed us. Tiernan realized that I had stopped, turned to look at me before he came toward me and ruffled my hair.

"It's okay, Trouble. This time, you are getting rewarded not punished. Trust me." He flashed me a big smile, one that made you feel all warm and tingly. Tiernan had asked me to trust him...

And I did trust him...

Nodding my head, I fell into step beside him and we carried on down the hall to the room that everyone called the wet room, because it was the only room with a drain for washing away the blood. Tiernan opened the door and motioned for me to go in and I did, glancing around to take in my surroundings.

The rest of Tiernan's unit, Aoife, Niamh, and James were all lined up to the side, observing the events happening in the room. The Rebel leaders all sat down as one of the older shoulders punched the traitor in the stomach and he groaned, falling to his knees, coughing.

"Simon Lane, you have been charged and convicted of murder and treason. You admitted your part in conspiring with angels and giving them knowledge that led to the death

of twelve of our soldiers. You offered no valid reason to explain your actions, and therefore, we the leaders of the Rebels have ruled that you are to die for your treasonous acts."

I felt the strength in Donnacha's words as he spoke, and I stood up a little taller. Something cold and metal touched my hand and I jerked my head to look at Tiernan, then down to the gun in his hand. I narrowed my gaze, not fully understanding why Tiernan was handing me a gun. I took it and held it in my grasp.

Then it dawned on me that I was to kill him.

I had known that this man betrayed us, but I also had known him since like forever. He'd brought candy apples back to me and Hayes one year. He'd helped repair the gates when they were knocked down in a storm. He had a sister who worked in the kitchens and a brother who had died during the first few years of the war.

"Raven."

I looked over at my mother, who beckoned me forward. I went to her, then she smiled at me, the smile of a soldier and not a mother and I was smart enough to know the difference in my mother's smiles after all these years.

"As the soldier who located the traitor, and stopped him from leaking any more information to the monsters who butchered our soldiers, we have decided to give you the honour of putting a bullet in his head."

Window dressing. That's what my mother's words were. And Tiernan had been wrong, I was being punished, though only me and the leaders would know that it wasn't a reward, but a penance. My loyalty was being tested as much as the traitor's had been. I was being given this task to see if I could execute someone I knew without flinching.

I had killed before, in the wastelands, and when an angel had been captured. I'd even managed to kill an angel in the field. It had been like a beautiful tragedy to see the angel fall from the sky, blood-soaked feathers, body broken as it crashed to the ground. I'd helped to protect the barracks when a rival group had tried to seize it for themselves.

Killing hadn't felt any different to me those times, and it wouldn't feel different this time around. I checked the safety on the gun, then strode right on up to where the man was on his knees before me and pressed the muzzle to his temple.

His eyes met mine and they widened with whatever he saw reflected there, though I know it wasn't emotion, because I had already put my emotions into a box and closed it while I performed my task, just like my mother had taught me to do.

He opened his mouth to say something and I pulled the trigger. The sound of the gunshot rang in my ears, as I turned, put back on the safety, and handed the gun to Tiernan, before I turned to face the leaders and saluted them.

Donnacha nodded his head in approval, then looked to Tiernan. "The girl is yours now. Train her, prepare her. Take her on missions with you. And continue to take Seamus' lad Hayes with you. He needs more hands-on experience. Dismissed."

We all saluted again, then everyone but the leaders, and the senior soldier, filed out of the room. Aoife and Niamh were speaking low, but I heard them say that they didn't need to babysit two teenagers who hadn't even hit puberty yet and they would be a liability.

The feelings I had shut away threatened to overflow, and my eyes burned with tears as the death I'd just administered sank into me. I wouldn't cry, not in front of my fellow soldiers, and I would never show them any signs of weakness. I numbed myself against the feelings, against the trauma, and instead I listened as Tiernan told me to be up and ready by six am for drills.

From that point on, I trained harder than anyone on my team. I made myself proficient in everything a soldier needed. I became indispensable and proved myself an asset to my unit. The next time I had to put a bullet in someone's head or cut a throat, I didn't so much as hesitate. I became the ultimate soldier, and I kept my emotions locked up tight.

It had been weeks before I had let myself feel anything but numb.

"Raven! Raven!" Nathaniel's raised voice startled me from my memories, but I remained where I was as he stormed into the bathroom, and I could see his boots as I kept my eyes firmly planted on the floor.

"What the hell were you thinking antagonising her like that? Taunting her like that? Have you lost your mind? Have you no bloody sense of your fragile human mortality?"

"Don't raise your fucking voice at me." I croaked out at Nathaniel, my voice sounding fragile and weak. "My head is pounding and I don't have the energy or the capacity to fight with you now. So, if you don't mind, you can come back and yell at me tomorrow."

"Were you crying?" Nathaniel asked me and when I

refused to answer him, Nathaniel stepped in front of me. "Please look at me."

I was feeling bratty, but I didn't have it in me to fight him. I looked up at Nathaniel's stupid handsome face through blurry eyes. In them I saw pity and disbelief, and I really wanted to punch him. I wanted to smack that pity right out of his eyes.

"What? Why does it make you look at me that way when you think I've been crying? Is it so hard to think that I might have a heart?" I beat my palm on my chest, hard enough for it to hurt. "Just because I'm a killer, doesn't mean I don't feel bad about it, ya know?"

Nathaniel stared at me for a moment, then knelt down in front of me and his nearness stirred something in me. I wanted to launch myself into his arms and have him hold me. I desperately needed the comfort of having someone be there for me. It was a weakness; this need I had. He reached out and tucked a strand of hair behind my ear, and I shivered at the ghost of his touch on my skin.

"What you did was grant that girl mercy, even in death. You were kind, and you were strong. You protected both the girl and Adriel."

"Noelle...her name was Noelle." I snapped at him, not really angry at him and Nathaniel knew it.

"Noelle. I won't forget again. I bet Noelle was grateful to be spared a painful death as much as Adriel is glad to be spared the burden of administrating the death. You protected them both when I could not."

I heard the pride in his voice, and it stabbed me

through the chest. Nathaniel was treating me like I was some sort of hero, and I was anything but a goddamn hero. My actions were not heroic...

Shame flooded through me and I tried to look down from the storm in his eyes but Nathaniel gripped my chin, keeping me from averting my gaze. My pulse raced at the heat in his eyes and I wondered if he could hear the rapid drumbeat of my foolish, stupid heart.

Nathaniel dipped his head lower, as if he meant to close the distance between us and I remembered the feel of his lips on mine, and my body thrummed with anticipation. I wanted to rid myself of the numbness. I wanted to feel something that wasn't pain, or guilt, or sadness.

"DANGER! DANGER!" The sound of Grainger's loud growled warning made Nathaniel jerk his hand away. He startled to his feet moments before the door swung open and Abraxas loomed in the doorway.

"Did I interrupt something? What a pity." His tone was droll and chiding, mocking us even after all that he had done. "Crying over the death of one little human, Raven? And here I was starting to think that you might actually have some fight in you. I liked it."

"Keep struggling. I like it."

I lifted my eyes to meet Abraxas' cold blue eyes, then looked at the remnants of his wings. The once beautiful snow-white plumage was riddled with charred feathers. His wings were pulled tightly against his back, and he looked at me without bothering to conceal his hatred for me.

"I like what you've done with your feathers. Looks

very shabby chic." I chuckled as he snarled, and took a step toward me but stopped when Nathaniel put a hand on his chest.

"What do you want, Abraxas? I told you to stay away from Raven." Nathaniel looked absolutely livid that Abraxas had the audacity to stride right on into my bedroom after everything that had happened, and look so damn pleased with himself for defying Nathaniel's order.

Abraxas snorted, folding his arms across his chest, though his smug expression didn't so much as falter. "Don't worry, Nate. I wouldn't be here if my Imperium hadn't sent me to fetch you, her only son. She would like a word with you. But I'll catch up with you soon, Raven."

"Not if I put a knife through your heart first, Brax. You've got to sleep some time. And you can't even fly this time round."

Abraxas pivoted with a snarl and left me and Nathaniel alone again. He looked at me, but I could tell that he didn't want to leave me all alone.

"Go. I'll be okay." I told him, the words tasting bitter on my tongue.

Lies. Lies. Lies. It was all a bunch of lies. I was not fine...

"I'd rather not leave you alone." Nathaniel told me and I knew he was stubborn enough to stay with me, even when it might piss off Rieka. Then again that might be an added bonus actually.

I sighed, then got to my feet, caught sight of myself in the mirror. My eyes were red and swollen, my skin blotchy, and my eyes looked pained and tired. Striding out passed Nathaniel, I walked over to the bed and climbed up on it.

Nathaniel emerged from the bathroom, hovered in the doorway as he kept his gaze firmly fixed on me. I rubbed my eyes and reached for a glass of water that was by my bed. I took a sip, then set it down, all while Nathaniel still looked at me.

"I'll be grand, Nate. I've got Grainger to mind me."

Nathaniel smiled, looking over at the gargoyle who seemed to puff out his chest. "I do not doubt that, however, I thought you might want to visit Adriel. He is quite upset that you were forced to act in his stead. It might offer him some comfort to know that you are okay."

I arched a brow at Nathaniel, surprised with his offer. "I admit that I expected you to go all alpha angel on me and demand that I do what you wanted and be like," I lowered my voice and tried to speak in Nathaniel's rumbly tone. "Raven, I am ordering you to stay in your room, and do not even dare attempt to leave or I will be forced to hunt you down and drag you back here, where I will stand and look stern while I lecture you on your mortality."

Nathaniel chuckled with laughter, a bemused look on his face. "Was that meant to be your impression of me?"

"Ya, it was. I think I nailed it, don't you?"

Nathaniel rolled his eyes before he said dryly. "Very accurate." He ran a hand through his dark hair. "I can walk you to Adriel's room if you like, before I go see what my mother wants?"

I shook my head, rolling my shoulders. "I think I'll take a shower before I go see him. If I go with all this cry face, he'll never believe me when I tell him that I'm okay with it all. I look a mess."

"I think you still look beautiful."

Now it was my turn to roll my eyes. "You need your eyes tested, Nate."

"My eyes are just fine, Raven."

Our gazes locked, and the tension seemed to suck all the air from the room. It crackled like the moment before a storm, when the air was thick, the skies darkened even more than usual, and the clouds were grey and ominous. If we came together now, it would be as devastating as a storm and over far too quickly for either of us to consider the damage it might have caused, to us, or to others.

"Adriel's room is through the courtyard, and off to the side. It's the only room at that end. Make sure that you go invisible while you make your way there. I'll be back as soon as I can."

And then Nathaniel was gone, closing the door, and leaving me to suck in a shaky breath. I was grateful for the reprieve. The last couple of days had been a lot, and to be fair, my head was all over the place and I needed to refocus and get some clarity. First, I needed to freshen up and go see Adriel, who was probably punishing himself as much as I was doing to myself right now.

After scrubbing myself in a shower and dressing in comfy clothes, I made my way to the kitchen first because I was starving. Pushing open the door to the kitchen, I paused when I saw Kalila tidying up. She was humming away, her back to me, and I knew if I didn't say anything I might startle her. I waited until she put down anything breakable before I cleared my throat.

Kalila whirled round with the grace of a dancer, her lips curving into a smile when she saw me. "Raven, come, come, let me get you something to eat."

I strode further into the kitchen area. "No, I can help myself. But you can sit with me while I eat if you want."

The angel frowned at me as I went to the pantry and took out some bread and meat and just put the meat in the bread and bit down as I walked back to the counter. Kalila had already made me a tea, and I thanked her, then told her to sit down with me.

She looked like she wanted to argue, but then

perched herself on the chair opposite me. We didn't say anything for the longest time and although it felt like Kalila wanted to say something to me, I gave her the space in the silence to decide that for herself.

"I think that you are very brave for what you did."

I let loose a snort, unsure which part of the last few days Kalila was referring to. The angel pursed her lips together in a frown and I set my mug down on the table. "I'm really not sure which part of the past few days you mean and I'm trying hard not to think too hard so you might need to elaborate."

Kalila twirled a finger around a strand of hair, her cheeks pinking. "For fighting off Abraxas. He might be a member of the League but I abhor any creature, angel or human, who could do such a crime to another person."

Lifting my gaze to Kalila, I understood her words and the numbness I'd been feeling subsided to be replaced by a rage for whatever monster had forced themselves on Kalila, the most sincere and good of any angel I had ever met. "Tell me who did it and I'll cut out their heart and give it to you."

Kalila blinked, then wet her lips. "You would do that without even knowing the story. You do not know me."

"In the months since I was dragged out of the abyss, you have treated me with nothing but kindness. You didn't look at me like I was human scum and I appreci-ated that. You might be too nice to seek revenge but I have no problem in doing it. And you don't have to tell me what happened."

"It was," Kalila said, looking out the window. I

wondered if what happened with Abraxas had triggered her, and she needed to explain to someone who had been through a similar experience so I let her, even if the memory was still sharp and jagged in my mind.

"A long time ago. We had only recently come to this world and I was oblivious to the many dangers. I had led a sheltered life in our world, protected first by Zadkiel and then Master Nathaniel. I did not understand the darkness in this world, in the people. It was my own fault for venturing out into the world without an escort."

It sickened my stomach to learn that Kalila had been hurt after coming to this world, and I wanted to cut the angel who hurt her to pieces.

"What happened, Kalila?" I encouraged her with softly spoken words.

"I cannot fly but I wanted to see this new world. I asked the League to accompany me but there was a skirmish with the Seraphan and there was no one around. The citadel had yet to be built and I ventured out into a wooded area. It was so dark and alluring. They trapped me in the middle of the forest, wanted to know if an angel tasted different."

Jesus Christ. How could she sit there and say it so calmly? How could she smile every day and flitter about the citadel like she was so happy? How the fuck did I not see the trauma in her?

"I was not brave like you, Raven. I lay there frozen beneath them. I forgot the training I had received as they invaded my body. I think they would have killed me if not for Cadoc."

That name...I'd heard it before from both Adriel and Nathaniel. He was a Seraphan who could amplify anger.

"I fear that Cadoc left much of his rage magic inside me because I don't ever feel not angry."

"One of the Seraphan rescued you?"

Kalila nodded her head, reaching out to pour herself a glass of water. "Yes. I had never liked violence but as I righted my skirt, I watched as Cadoc ripped those men apart and scattered their limbs around the forest. I was terrified that he might hurt me too, and yet, his rage was directed toward the humans and not me. He was... gentle with me. He carried me back to the camp, covered in the blood of the human men, holding a white cloth until he had safely handed me over to the League."

"I am truly sorry that happened to you."

"As I am sorry for what happened to you."

We sat in silence as I finished my tea, then I asked her. "Have you seen Cadoc since that day?"

Kalila's eyes widened as she shook her head. "Oh no. He is Seraphan. It is forbidden. Though I must admit that I do wish I could thank him for coming to my aid. He no doubt saved my life."

Cadoc might be Seraphan, but he had already gone up a step in my estimation for how he had treated Kalila. She popped off her chair then, and came round to rest her hand on my arm. "Do not make my burden yours to carry. You carry too much as it is. There are monsters in this world, both human and angel, but it makes me happy to know that there are humans like you, or angels like Nathaniel and even Cadoc, who are heroic. Good-night Raven."

I lingered in the kitchen for a long time after that, mulling about Kalila's words.

There are monsters in this world, both human and angel.

Kalila thought me a hero... but I was just a different kind of monster.

Leaving the kitchen, I made my way down the hall, pulling my power to me as I walked out into the courtyard. I looked up to the sky, breathing in the chill of the night air, standing in the exact spot Abraxas and I had fought and I let myself think of myself as heroic for just a minute.

I felt a sense of wrongness in the air a moment before a scream ripped through the night and I took off in a run toward Adriel's room. Shoving open the door, I blinked my eyes a few times to try and adjust to the darkness. Adriel lay on a pallet on the floor, a solitary blanket covering his lower half as he held his hands up as if he was blocking an attacker.

He screamed again, his eyes snapping open, pure black as he shouted at someone to stop. He grabbed at his head, crying out, the black veins pulsing from his eyes. It was obvious that Adriel was trapped inside a nightmare, that the events of the last couple of days had not only triggered me, but Kalila, and Adriel as well.

I took stock of Adriel as I inched closer, saying his name but that did little to snap him out of the past. I'd never seen Adriel without a shirt before, and the scars on his torso were way worse than the ones to his face and arms. They were similar to my own, but considering an angel's healing abilities, the torture must have been horrific and daily to sustain this kind of scarring.

"Raisel," Adriel moaned, his body jerking. "My love. Save me, please."

Jesus, the pain in his tone was way worse than looking at his scars.

I took a step closer, then dropped to my knees in front of him. "Adriel, it's me, Raven. Time to wake up now."

Those black eyes focused on me, then snapped out to grab my wrists with a snarl. I yanked my arms, trying to get out of his grip, but he held on tightly. The veins slithered down his jaw, his throat and then his arms, before I felt this emptiness crawl over my skin and felt the blood trickle from my nose.

"Adriel! Wake the fuck up or you are going to kill me!" I shouted at him and somehow it jostled him from sleep, the black receding back up his limbs until green eyes looked back at me. His gaze dropped to the blood that was still trickling from my nose.

"Oh fuck, Raven." Adriel let go of my hands, and I fell back on my ass as he slammed himself against the wall. "I dreamt I was back in their clutches. I dreamt that Raisel was the one hurting me."

I had always thought that Adriel was this force of strength, that he had survived when not many could have. We were always meant to be kindred spirits, but I had never seen him look so utterly depleted, so fragile and vulnerable.

Swiping the blood from my nose with my sleeve, I crawled next to him on the pallet and reached up to run my fingers through his hair. "Shhh, it's okay. It was just a nightmare. I got you."

Adriel shifted to lay his head in my lap, and I just sat there, running my fingers through his hair in the darkness, neither of us uttering a syllable. I could feel Adriel's heavy breathing, the hurried way in which his chest rose and fell, like he was struggling to stay calm.

"When I was younger," I began, keeping my fingers in his curly hair. "I had a terrible temper. I know, I know. Very hard to believe with how calm and refined I am now, right?"

Adriel snorted, but his breathing was starting to go back to normal so I went on. "I always knew I was different, not like others my age. And some of the children were afraid of me, and they used to make up stories that when it was night and all the candles were blown out, that I made myself invisible to hunt little children and give them to the monsters in the dark to feed."

The monster in the dark was always me...

"It upset me at first, because I always thought the dark wasn't something to be afraid of. But then again, I never feared a monster under the bed, or one in the wardrobe because the monster in the dark was always me. I told my mother this and that it had made me angry, at the children, at the other adults for not contradicting them, and finally my mother, for adding fuel to the fire."

I swallowed hard, the dart in my chest hurting so fucking much. "But my mother just lay her palm on my cheek before she said. 'Raven, you must learn to wield the fire inside you so fiercely that after a while, the dark begins to fear you.' She didn't care that I had no friends because all that mattered to her was that I was feared."

"Your mother sounds like a bitch." Adriel mumbled as he lifted his head and sat up, leaning against the wall.

"She is."

"Our mother died when we were born." Adriel told me, his bare shoulder brushing mine. "Angelic births are difficult. And twins are a rarity. Our father raised us. He was a soldier in Zadkiel's League and when our powers manifested as healing rather than fighting, he handed off our training to Verena's mother, who was a healer."

"That must have been hard." I said in response.

"It was the way of angels." Adriel huffed out a breath. "It was the same way when Verena was given to the League because her parents did not know how to raise a warrior child. We spent half our time with Verena's mother and half our time training with the League."

"Ya know, I find it hard to imagine you as a child. That's weird right?"

Adriel chuckled softly. "No. Sometimes, it's hard to remember the boy, the man I once was. Adair had always been the quieter of the two of us. More even tempered. More naïve, you could say. I was curiouser. I was hungry to learn, and absorb any knowledge I could. And I was Adair's older brother, it was my job to protect him."

"I bet he hated that."

"No, the opposite in fact," Adriel mused, and I could hear the fondness in his tone. "It amused him with how

142

overprotective I was of him. Suitors had to get passed me if they wanted to court him. I knew that the lover he chose would have to be strong enough to protect him when I wasn't there so that was how I vetted them. Adair never once complained, just reminded me that we had the same face and I also had angels vying to share my bed. However, I only had eyes for one angel."

"Raisel."

"Yes."

I didn't pry or attempt to delve deeper into Adriel's painful memories, but it would seem that tonight was the night that everyone felt like sharing their stories with me.

"I first saw her in the forest, because that was where Ray felt most at home. Her power is tied to nature; she can manipulate plants and vegetation. Make it bend to her will. I walked into the forest and she was just lying there, on her back, her fingers dug into the dirt, her eyes closed. Her hair was the same green as the grass, her wings too, and when she opened her eyes to look at me, those eyes too blended in with the forest floor."

Adriel laughed and I found it hard to understand how he could still think of the angel who had captured his heart and used it to trap him, and still laugh.

"Was it love at first sight?"

"Heavens, no," Adriel barked out a laugh. "We hated one another. She was such a soldier, a warrior that the opinions of a healer mattered little to her. What is the odd phrase you humans have? There is a fine line between love and hate? Yes, that describes the early days of me and Raisel. It was only when I had injured myself sparring with Makata that Raisel stormed into the infirmary to yell at me for getting hurt. I kissed her to shut her up."

I let loose a snort. "Did she punch you for kissing her?"

Adriel rubbed the back of his head. "Eh, no."

That made me bark out a laugh. "Adriel!"

"As I said, there is a fine line between love and hate. It was maddening how quickly we fell. How intertwined we became. For nearly a century we loved one another and then she served me up on a platter like we had never been lovers, never been almost mated."

I knew mated meant something to the angels like marriage to humans, but I'd never known that Adriel and this Raisel had been that close to making it official.

"I divulge too many of our ways, I fear. The nightmare has made me complacent."

I shrugged, nudging Adriel with my shoulder. "Who am I gonna tell? And what strategic advantage would I gain by telling your story? It's not all that exciting anyways."

Adriel laughed, shaking his head. "I have no response to that."

"Made ya laugh though so my work it done."

Adriel fell silent after that, before he rested his hand over where mine lay on my knee. It was a familial gesture, and I turned my head to look at him.

"I do not think that I could have survived using my powers against that poor girl. I should feel selfish for the relief and gratitude I feel toward you, Raven. I feel that shying away from my own darkness has only added to yours."

"I'm tough. I can take it."

"Neither of us should have to be tough and carry it. But you did deserve to know that I am grateful to you."

I don't say anything then, just look away from the intensity in his gaze. "I think I preferred it when you were beating me up. I'm not built for all this mushy girly sharing crap."

"Then tomorrow we can pretend this never happened and return to some semblance of normality."

"Sounds fucking good to me."

I push off the pallet, and get to my feet, pausing to look down at Adriel. "If you want to prove to people that you did more than survive what happened to you, that you are more than someone they need to watch out for, if you want Adair to stop looking at you with cautious eyes and remind him of the big brother who chased off admirers, then you need to start living again."

Adriel didn't say anything so I went on. "Stop hiding out down here and reclaim a room. Sleep in a proper bed. Stop isolating yourself from the League and just maybe, they will look at you and not see the scars, the trauma. Remind them of the Adriel that you were before the world tried to break you, and if that's not possible, then show them that it's okay to be the Adriel that you are now, because I think he's pretty great. Laugh and play, and do whatever the fuck you want to do. You win every time when you wake up in the morning and choose to live, choose to dream of better days."

"It's hard to sell dreams to someone who has walked through nightmares."

I walked over to the door as Adriel spoke, opening the door before I peered over my shoulder. "Ya, it is. But what is a nightmare but a scary fucking dream. It's still a dream. It's still something you are capable of, Adriel. Don't forget that."

T he next couple of days passed by without much incident, and I was glad for the little reprieve. I couldn't help the smile on my lips the next day when Adriel asked Nathaniel if he could allocate him a room in the League sleeping quarters, with Nathaniel clasping him on the shoulder and telling him that he always had a room, right next door to Adair.

I offered to help Adriel move in to his new room but the angel had rolled his eyes while telling me that he had little personal belongings and only a few items of clothing. He seemed at ease with his decision, though I still stayed awake the entire first night in case the nightmares tried to chase away this massive step forward.

I'd been sitting invisible outside my bedroom door, watching as angels came and went from their rooms, until Nathaniel came up the steps, spotted me and narrowed his gaze. I'd held up my finger to my lips as he came to sit down beside me, the slant of his wing brushing against my shoulder. Letting go of my power, the stealth gone since dumbass next to me decided to join in on my watch.

"What has you sitting out here in the dead of night?" Nathaniel asked, pulling one knee up and resting his hands on it.

"Adriel," I answered, glancing to the door at the farthest end of the landing. "I wanted to make sure that he was okay, so I couldn't sleep. Nightmares can be a right bitch."

Nathaniel didn't respond, just sat beside me, and I wondered what nightmares this angel who confused the hell out of me had.

"If you were Nathaniel, what would you be most afraid of?"

Verena had said that to me when I had asked her to tell me what Nathaniel's greatest fear was. It made sense, it really did, because whenever I taunted him and called him a monster, I could see how much it hurt him. Some of our fears were similar, because I was afraid of becoming my mother also, though, I think I was more afraid of becoming the monster she raised me to be.

"You're quiet tonight."

"You say that like it's a bad thing." I remarked with a snort, running my hand through my hair.

"I didn't say it was a bad thing, just noting that you were quiet."

His teasing tone told me that he was relaxed tonight, so I shoved at his shoulder as I rolled my eyes. "Bastard."

Nathaniel chuckled, and fell silent again.

"I never thought to ask you, how do you know when I use my power? What does it look like to you?"

Ducking his head, Nathaniel cleared his throat before he spoke. "I can feel your power. I can feel it in your bones when its active. When you disappear, you become blurry around the edges. It's like your power is trying to make me not see you, but I do."

"Huh." Was all I had said back to him.

Nathaniel had pushed off the floor, looking down at me as he held out his hand to help me up. I took his hand, was yanked off the floor so quickly I had to put my hand on Nathaniel's chest to steady myself before ripping it away like I'd been burnt.

"Adriel has a shift in an hour or so. Go get some sleep, Raven. Be ready after lunch tomorrow."

That was all Nathaniel had said before he turned and strode away, heading not into his own bedroom but back down the steps and out of view. With a sigh, I headed into my room, and had thrown myself on the bed and crashed with Grainger snoring beside me.

The following afternoon I stood in the courtyard, my axe at my waist. I was dressed in cargo pants, a long-sleeved t-shirt and a hooded black jumper. I wasn't sure what Nathaniel had planned for us, but in order to be prepared, I had tamed my hair up in a braid. On my feet I wore sturdy boots.

As I waited for the commander of the League to make his appearance, I kept myself occupied by throwing some of Asterin's throwing stars at the target. I did that for about an hour and was just about to give up the ghost and head back inside when Nathaniel barrelled out through the double doors. His face was filled with anger and he looked like he wanted to rip someone's head off.

For a moment, fear crashed over me and all I could think was that he knew what I was.

"I want to hear you say it. I want to hear it from your own lips. What are you, Raven?"

For a moment, it seemed like the entire world fell away and it was just me and Nathaniel left, not even the weather dared to interfere as I wet my lips and told him. "I'm a Nephilim. I'm half angel."

He growled at me, the fingers on my chin tightening. "A filthy half-breed with deceit in her blood. You fooled us all, Raven. And now I will put an end to your pitiful existence. And if you needed any proof as to why we are monsters, this will surely be enough..."

Nathaniel growled, an animalistic rumble in his chest, as he lifted his eyes to me. I had taken my axe from my waist, poised for him to attack me, and his gaze narrowed as he took in my stance, my weapon. When he took a step forward, I retreated.

"What the hell is wrong with you?"

"There's murder in your eyes, Nate."

Slamming his eyes shut, Nathaniel gave me his back and I looked at those wonderful obsidian wings of his and the tightness in his shoulders. If I could get the jump on him, I could severe the scapula on one of his wings and that might slow him down. I felt this eery sense of calm flood through me and it amused me just how thinking about spilling blood put me at ease.

Slowly, Nathaniel turned back to me, his eyes and expression no longer filled with rage. Instead, it was replaced with a mask I knew too well, the one where he was hiding exactly how he was feeling when he wanted to appear like he had his shit together.

It wasn't dissimilar to the mask I wore from time to time.

"You can put the axe away, Raven. I don't plan on killing you today."

"Well, that's very fucking reassuring, Nate." His expression was grim, even as I stowed my axe on the belt around my waist, then folded my arms across my chest. "What has your knickers in a twist?"

"It doesn't matter." He ground out bluntly and I let loose an exasperated breath.

"Riiiight," I drawled, then shook my head. "If you're gonna be a miserable bastard for the afternoon, I think I'd rather not hang out so I'll be on my way."

"No." Nathaniel growled, stepping to block my escape. "You and I have somewhere to be. Let's go."

Nathaniel is walking out the double doors before I can even open my mouth and he left me with no choice but to traipse after him, his angry strides making it hard for me to catch him up without jogging after him. Just as it appeared that Nathaniel is leading me down the corridor to the throne room, and my heart sinks, he veered off to the right, leading me down a corridor that I had never been down before.

The silence made the rapid beat of my heart seem even louder, and I wondered if Nathaniel could hear just how much it thundered inside my chest. We seemed to walk for a long time, and still Nathaniel had yet to utter a word to me.

"Where are we going, Nate?"

"You'll see."

Infuriating asshole.

I heard him chuckle like I had said the words out loud, but he knew me well enough to know that his withholding information would annoy the hell out of me. And he was fucking right, it did annoy the hell out of me.

We came to the end of the corridor so suddenly that it surprised me. The door looked medieval, with wood and bolts to keep it locked. Nathaniel shifted the locks, then slid the bolt across and made to open the door, looking back at me. Then he stepped back and motioned with his head.

"After you, Raven."

I shot him a suspicious glare, and Nathaniel chuckled, easing some of the tension that had a vice grip on my neck and shoulders. I shoved at the heavy door, pushing it open and took a step as it did, then froze.

Nothing but green surrounded me, making my heart clench. The moment I had stepped outside the door, my feet trampled the grass. I ventured out a little more, then inhaled through my nose. I could scent the flowers around me, I could scent the grass. I looked at the trees and saw the remnants of the yellow and red leaves that had fallen during the autumn season. Rushing forward, I peered over my shoulder at Nathaniel as he stepped outside and closed the door behind us, and just waited while I soaked it in.

I took in all of my surroundings, then looked behind Nathaniel and sucked in a breath when I lifted my gaze to travel up the tall bricks that surrounded us. I was outside. I was not just outside. I was outside the goddamn citadel!

My first instinct was to run. Of course it was and Nathaniel could see it in my eyes.

"If you run, if I have to chase you, that's it Raven. I will have to lock you back in the prison. That was the boon I made in order to bring you with me today."

I thought back on his anger when I first saw him, his foul humour and I knew he had gone to the head bitch in charge to get permission to take me outside the walls. Rieka had expected me to bolt at the first opportunity and I would hand her the reason to lock me up again. The temptation was still there though as I tried to get a grasp of my surroundings to know where we were and where the nearest Rebel safehouse was.

"I won't run, I promise. Not unless my life is in danger and I have no choice but to do so in order to stay alive. You have my word."

Nathaniel held my gaze for a second, then nodded, before striding down the little hill to a small pathway, and I stayed where I was. "Wait, we are going farther away from the citadel?"

"Yes, now hurry up. We are already running late."

I spared one last look at the walls of the citadel, then hurried after Nathaniel, jogging until I reached him and fell into step beside him. "If you are in such a rush, why didn't you just fly?"

Nathaniel looked over at me. "Would you like to fly with me, Raven?"

Yes, yes, fucking hell yes!

That was what I wanted to say but I kept that to myself. Instead, I rolled my eyes. "Nope. Not in the slightest. It just seems stupid to be walking about out here when anyone can see you, when you could fly up there and be safe."

"Everyone expects an angel to fly, but they never expect them to walk and therefore, they don't watch the roads. I have walked this path many a time and have yet to be set upon. Though now the Rebel assassin knows another one of my secrets."

"Not very juicy information to find out the commander of the League of Dominious likes to frolic in the wilderness. And I don't even know where we are. My internal compass is all screwed up."

"North, we are headed north."

"Toward the bloody Seraphan?"

Nathaniel cocked a brow. "Afraid of a little danger?"

I smiled as I rolled my eyes. "What do you think? But even I can't kill all the Seraphan single-handed."

"Hopefully there will be no need for that. Talk to me about Ireland."

"What do you want to know? I doubt there's much that you don't know by now."

Nathaniel didn't say anything then, as we walked through the rubble of an abandoned town, my eyes scanning round like I was expecting an ambush, though I wasn't sure if it would be human or Seraphan. I didn't have a clue what to tell Nathaniel as we crossed through the town and back onto a grassier area.

A shriek ripped through the air, and I whirled round, my axe already in my hand. I heard a keening sound again, and it sent a shudder through me. "Wastelander."

"It is rare that one ventures up this far but they do on occasion. One of the soldiers on patrol will take care of it."

It – like the creature hadn't once been human, hadn't once been someone's something; a mother, father, sister, brother, son or daughter. Just another victim of the angels here in this world.

A flicker of disgust must have crossed my face because Nathaniel frowned. "What?"

"It." I responded, sheathing my axe and walking forward again. "Does it even matter to you lot that the reason why so many humans turned into mindless cannibals was because of something to do with your arrival? It's like the electricity going out...the waste-landers are as much a direct result of the angels as the power going out."

Nathaniel fell into step with me again and he sighed. "I apologize. I meant no offence. But yes, we are aware that something in the frequency of our bodies caused misfires in some human brains and they became what you call wastelanders. We believe it's the same occurrence as to why the electricity stopped working."

I was mildly surprised that Nathaniel and the angels

had investigated the wastelanders, though it didn't stop the thought from popping into my head that they had only done so because if they could find a cure for the disease in the brains of the wastelanders, that was more humans for them to own.

"I know people who have lost parents, siblings, lovers to the wastelands. We found as many as we could and put them out of their misery. Others, we couldn't locate. They must be deeper in the caverns than we can go. I tried once, to go down into the caverns, but there was too many wastelanders down there that if my power failed, I'd have been eaten alive."

We came to a hill, and climbed up it, the long blades of grass as high as my knees as we came to the top and I blinked before letting loose a laugh. Nestled on the top of the hill was a church, a tiny unsuspecting church that had holes in the roof and the windows were shattered.

Lifting my brows, I glanced over at Nathaniel. He shrugged his shoulders, and headed for the church, weaving around gravestones, as a shriek sounded in the distance and I shivered, glancing back down the hill before I followed after Nathaniel.

"Not that I don't appreciate the little trip away from the citadel, but why the hell are we here? I mean, you can see the irony or the humour in this right? An angel bringing me to a church? There has got to be some joke about this, right?"

Nathaniel stepped into the archway of the church, before standing sideways, his hands pressed to his stomach. "I want to show you that the world isn't black and white, Raven. There are shades of grey that even that twisted mind of yours can't predict. When you had your nightmare before Abraxas attacked you, it was me that haunted your dreams, am I right?"

My heart was lodged in my throat, so all I could do was nod.

"And yet, after Abraxas attacked you, there were no nightmares. You're still not really afraid of him, but something has made you very afraid of me. I want...no, that's wrong. I *need* for you to understand that I am not a monster and that the things I do, are to protect those I care for. Even if doing some it kills a part of me with the consequences."

"Everything I put you through, Raven, it is to protect you. You must believe that."

My mother's voice ran through my mind, and I closed my eyes to keep Nathaniel from seeing the hurt in them. "You might believe that, but it doesn't make it all true. The decisions any leader makes impacts those around them. If you think that your actions only affect you in the long run, then you are already heading down a path there might not be a way back from. But I'm not a leader...I'm just a soldier. A weapon."

Nathaniel didn't say anything so I shook my head and headed into the church. Pigeons flew around the rafters as I walked in, Nathaniel hot on my heels. Rows of broken pews led the way up to the alter, and even that had crackled marble, right down the centre where the cross was. The stained-glass windows cast shadows on the ground, well the ones that were still intact anyway.

I strode up to the altar and bend down to pick up a cross that had been knocked from somewhere and set it down on the steps as I turned round to look at Nathaniel. He flared out his wings, and the image of an actual angel standing in the aisle of the church, his black wings spread out like an angel of darkness was an image I would never forget.

He shot me a bemused look, then glanced over to the confessional box, then back at me. I was suddenly hyper aware that there had to be a reason why Nathaniel had dragged me here this afternoon. I spared a glance toward the confessional, heard Nathaniel ask me to have an open mind, as the door creaked open, and a figure stepped out to join this little shindig.

FOURTEEN

An angel I had never seen before stepped out of the confessional; her face covered in what looked like a bandana. Her gaze slid to mine and then to Nathaniel as I heard her say. "I didn't think you were coming."

"We were running a little behind schedule. You are well?"

"I'm okay. This must be the infamous Raven Cassidy I've heard so much about."

She pulled down her bandana, and smiled, though I did not return it.

Her eyes were the colour of the dark stems of grass we had waded through to get to the church, her hair the same. Her wings were also the same colour as her hair and eyes, and without even hearing her name, I knew who this bitch was.

"Her hair was the same green as the grass, her wings too, and when she opened her eyes to look at me, those eyes too blended in with the forest floor."

Anger flared in my chest as I came back down the aisle, the traitorous bitch eyeing me wearily until I stood halfway between her and Nathaniel. My hand wrapped around the hilt of my axe, and I had the weapon ready as Nathaniel, who seemed oblivious to the sudden hostility in the air started to speak.

"Raven, this is Raisel. Ray, this is Rave-"

I launched myself at Raisel before his sentence was done, slashing the axe across her stomach, and she hissed, taking to the air as the scent of her blood made me smile. Nathaniel barked out my name and I ignored him, as I hoisted up my axe to throw right at Raisel.

"If I ever see the bitch that hurt you, I'll gut her. I would make sure that she felt every bit of pain and anguish that she inflicted on you."

That was the promise that I had given to Adriel months ago and I would deliver on that promise today. I reached inside my pocket and flung a throwing star at Raisel and she darted to the side, quicker than any angel I had seen before. Then ground rumbled underneath my feet ands I had a second to jerk sideways as roots shot up from the ground.

"Stop, Raven. Stop this right now."

I ignored Nathaniel as he came forward to try and wrap his arm around my waist and pull me back. I side stepped him, kicking his leg, watching it buckle as he swore. I hopped up on one of the pews, pulled on all of my strength and made to leap up, axe in hand when something thick wrapped around my leg and slammed me down to the ground.

My back hit the tile hard, the air leaving my lungs as I tried to jerk into a sitting position, but found that I couldn't. Thick roots had ensnared my arms and legs, pinning me to the ground. I snarled, trying to swing the axe at the bindings. Nathaniel grabbed my axe from me and I growled at him.

"Let me up! Let me fucking up and I'm gonna cut out that bitch's heart for what she did to Adriel. Then I'll take great pleasure in telling him that I made good on my promise to him."

Nathaniel stood over me as Raisel lowered herself to the ground, the two of them sharing a glance. Her eyes were filled with remorse, not that I cared. I only cared about avenging Adriel.

"What did you promise Adriel, Raven."

I laughed, then flashed Raisel a feral grin. "I told him that if I ever laid eyes on the bitch that hurt him, I'd gut her. I would make sure that she felt every bit of pain and anguish that she inflicted on him. And that I could do it, without flinching."

Raisel folded her arms across her chest. "I can see why you like her, Nathaniel. She has fire in her."

"Too fucking much most of the time." Nathaniel said dryly, and I gave him a one finger salute that made Raisel laugh.

Frustration surged through me and then I remembered Nathaniel's diary, remembered that not only was Raisel the lover who had betrayed Adriel, she was also Asterin's sister.

Asterin's mood darkens when someone mentions Raisel, their sisterly bond cut because of the war.

"You might want to go fetch that throwing star for me, Raisel, or else I'll have to explain to Az how and why I lost it."

The bitch flinched when I used the shortened version of her sister's name and I smirked. I might not be able to make her bleed with my axe right now, but I could still cut her deep on the inside.

"Jesus, you really are a vicious bitch."

"You have no fucking idea. Tell your plants to let me go and I can show you just how vicious I can be."

"Enough!" Nathaniel roared and it was loud enough to make the windows tremble. "You two are giving me a migraine. Raisel, let Raven go and Raven will behave. You have my word."

"He doesn't speak for me." I snarled as the roots unwrapped themselves from my wrists and ankles. I scrambled to my feet, reached out to Nathaniel to take my axe, but he wouldn't give it back to me.

"There are things you need to listen to first, then you can have your weapon back. Now sit down. You too, Raisel."

I wanted to buck against the order in his tone as Raisel lowered herself to one of the pews, her eyes on me the entire time as Nathaniel grabbed my shoulders and all but shoved me down on one of the pews, before sitting in the pew in between me and Raisel.

"Is this where you tell me that you've been pretending not to be a Seraphan all this time and are secretly working with Ascian still in order to kill your mother, because I might actually reign in my murderous tendencies for just a minute if it means cutting out your mother's cold, dead heart."

Raisel's eyes widened as she glanced from me to Nathaniel, who just rubbed his temple, like he did have a migraine. Served the prick right.

"I am not a secret Seraphan, Raven. In fact, it's quite the opposite in fact. Raisel is my spy within the Seraphan. She always has been."

Jesus fucking Christ, Raisel was Nathaniel's spy! I had known that he had someone in their camp feeding him information, and that Ascian had someone in Nathaniel's feeding him information, but I never considered it would be one of the League itself that was the angel behind enemy lines.

As soon as the shock of it wore off and I could think clearly, something struck me and I snapped my gaze to Nathaniel's. "Please tell me that you didn't have a heads up that Ascian was going to take Adriel? Please tell me that all this time, while the pain of her betrayal had been eating at Adriel, that the angel who had a hand in it all along was not standing beside him pretending to be his goddamn friend?"

I saw no remorse in Nathaniel's face as he simply stated. "It was the lesser of two evils. The Seraphan had not wanted to take Adriel. I simply made it impossible for them to take the twin that would not have survived their savagery. Adriel could and he did."

I bolted upright in the pew and walked away from

them, the need for violence so overwhelming in me that I had to put some distance between me and them or I would explode. "Adriel might have technically survived, Nathaniel, but he lives with what he has become every day and you did that too him. You did. How could you both do that to him?"

"Had we told Adriel what it was we intended to do, he would have offered to do it himself for Adair. Of that I have no doubt." Raisel said, a fondness in her tone that she didn't deserve.

Pointing my finger at her, I growled. "You can shut the fuck up. I won't be responsible for what I do if I have to listen to you tell me that it was for the best."

"Raven," Nathaniel chastised, and drawing the intensity of my rage back to him. "Adair was their target because Ascian knew that out of the two healers, Adair was the weaker twin. He was softer than Adriel back then, and if the Seraphan had taken Adair, both brothers would have been broken. It was the only mercy we could offer, to save Adair, and give them Adriel instead."

I was quiet for a moment, then I recalled something Adair had said to me when he was speaking about Adriel. "It's not always just the heart. Sometimes, your mind breaks as well."

Raisel looked away from me. Good. Let it sink in that she had not only broken his heart, but helped break his mind as well. I was still looking at her when she turned back to me, the jealously in her tone unmistakable.

"Just how close are you with Adriel?"

I wanted to antagonize her, and maybe Nathaniel as

well. I wanted to needle Raisel since I couldn't make her bleed. "Wouldn't you like to know. I can tell you how firm his grip is. I can tell you where the worst of his scars are on his bare torso. I can tell you about the chords of muscles in his arms and even the scent on his skin when he's all hot and sweaty."

That dragged a growl from Raisel, and I let loose a chortle of laughter when Nathaniel told me that was enough. "Raven is trying to get to you. Yes, she has a bond with Adriel, but it is sisterly in nature."

"Bonding over a shared experience of being tortured will bring two people intimately close together."

"Do you think it was easy for me to stand back and watch the angel I loved being tortured? Every strike, every time he begged me to help him, I almost broke and went to him. If I showed the slightest emotion, Ascian would have figured out that I was the spy and he'd have put my head on a spike for it."

"I still might do that." I told her, getting me another glare from Nathaniel.

"Ray, have you got anything to report?"

Her green eyes drifted over to study me. "Are you sure I should be reporting to you with her here?"

"Just report, Raisel."

Raisel wet her lips, then sighed. "Ascian has been even more secretive of late. The only ones he seems to keep in confidence are Cadoc and Takara. I heard that Cadoc had been trying to lure some non-league soldiers to Ascian's side. Niran is still being kept away from nearly everyone, but I did get close enough to get a visual on him two nights ago. Ascian still has him."

She glanced at me, then back at Nathaniel. "Somehow, probably from his own spies, Ascian has heard about the human helping Rieka weed out the spies in her citadel." Raisel paused when I snorted at the thought that I would really be helping Rieka.

"He's...intrigued. He asked Cadoc how easy would it be to extract Raven from the citadel, but Cadoc said that would be hard because she is never alone. Ascian wanted it confirmed that it was true that Raven had a temper, one that Cadoc could exploit, and while I can't confirm that to Ascian, I can see that they might be able to."

It was Nathaniel's turn to snort this time, and I shot him an annoyed glare, making him chuckle. He ran a hand through his hair, his laughter dying out. "Can you get to Niran and get him to leave with you?"

"Nope. It seems like him and Khione have started to feel something for one another. He won't go without her and she is loyal to Ascian. Though it could be Niran working an angle."

Nathaniel got to his feet, paced for a bit. "I ask this of you every time we meet, but do you want to come home? Are you in danger?"

Raisel offered him a sad smile. "Considering Raven's reaction, I think I'd be in more danger returning home than I am with Ascian. And that would compromise you too, Nathaniel. They all need to think that I am still the bitch who led Adriel to his capture, and turned my back on them. Until the day the Seraphan are defeated, that is the role I must play."

"And you play it so well." I couldn't help but inform her, but neither she nor Nathaniel even looked at me.

"That would be my cross to bear, Raisel. I have played the villain before and if you want to come home, then I will play it again."

"Every good story needs a villain, and I am sorry if I am the villain in your story."

Nathaniel had said that to me not long after he offered me a route out of the prison. He had been standing in my room, his room, as I stripped off my clothes and he had said to me in a sad tone that had made my heart clench, that he was sorry if he was the villain in my story.

It would seem, to Nathaniel, that he was the villain in his own story too.

"Have you got something that I can give Ascian as a reason why I was out today? I told him that I was meeting an informant."

"Tell Ascian that there are rumours in the citadel that I am starting to show signs of rebellion against the Imperium. Tell him that there has been a number of times where we can be heard arguing quite loudly in the throne room."

I absorbed that information, because it didn't sound like a lie as Raisel got to her feet before she asked. "If Ascian tries to verify the information?"

"It's the truth. We argued even this morning. I have made no qualms about how little I have approved of her actions of late. The gossip circles are having a field day. Just yesterday I overheard someone wonder if I was going to challenge her for Imperium."

"Are you?" I blurted out, eager to know if that was something Nathaniel would do.

"Not yet." Was all he said and that wasn't really a no.

"I'll head back now." Raisel said, keeling her eyes on me as she came up and embraced Nathaniel, who then kissed her forehead.

"Stay safe, Ray. Send word if you need to see me before the next check in."

"I will." Raisel turned to me, and I arched a brow in challenge as she said. "You won't believe me but I do love him, Adriel."

"I think the idiot still loves you too, for what it's worth."

Wetness made her eyes shine. "It is worth more than you will know."

I didn't say anything else until long after Raisel was gone and Nathaniel had flown up to retrieve the throwing star I'd managed to lodge in the ceiling. He handed me my axe and the throwing star, his face stern as he told me. "You cannot tell Adriel that Raisel is my spy."

"I won't keep this from him. I can't."

"Adriel is an honourable angel. He will defy any orders I give him and try and save Raisel. Your assessment is correct. He still loves her and she him. He would unleash his anger or Cadoc would do it for him and inadvertently kill anyone in the vicinity, Raisel included.

There would be no pulling him out of the depths of his darkness. Not even you could do it."

He's right...I fucking hate it but Nathaniel is right and he knows that I know it. He's backed me into a corner with this knowledge, and now by letting me in on his secret, Nathaniel had made me his accomplice and I had to withhold the truth from everyone, but especially from Adriel.

"You bastard. You complete and utter shithead. You've made me complicit. You manoeuvred this so that I would know all of this fucking farce and be unable to tell anyone because you knew that I would rather keep your lies to myself than hurt Adriel."

Nathaniel shook his head, advancing a step, and I backed away, the anger making me tremble so much that if he touched me, I'd unleash my wrath on him. He must have seen it in my face because he halted, before saying, "I can see how you would see it that way, but all I wanted to do was show you that there are many moving parts, Raven. More than you know."

"I don't think I want to know anymore."

His shoulders sagged as I brushed passed him and headed for the door. Raisel was long gone and I was glad for it, my anger at her still not quenched. The dark of winter began to descend, ready to plunge the already ashen skies into oblivion. I made to head back the way we came, needing to put some distance between us.

"Raven, we have one more stop to make before we return to the citadel."

"What?" I tossed at him in a snarky tone. "You gonna

bring me to another church and Ascian's gonna stride out and you two are gonna bro hug?"

"Bro hug?"

"You know, that awkward thing men do when they hug and pat each other on the back like they are congratulating each other for having a penis."

Nathaniel looked at me, then burst out laughing, bending over at the waist. I must have amused him greatly with how hard he was yanking it up. "Your mind is a very strange place, Raven Cassidy."

I flipped him off, waiting until he had gotten his composure in check again and placed my hands on my hips. "Can we just get this over with?"

"So eager to return to the citadel?" Nathaniel queried, heading down the opposite side of the hall and I had no choice but to follow him.

"No. I'm just not ready for any more surprises you might want to spring on me. It's making me want to shoot my shot and see if I could outrun you."

FIFTEEN

N athaniel ground to a halt so suddenly I almost ran into the back of him. I'd only been slightly serious about taking a chance and getting the hell out of dodge, but apparently Nathaniel thought that I actually gonna give it a try. I did have form so I couldn't really fault him for thinking about it.

"I was joking, Nate, relax."

"Do you know what she would make me do if you did run?" Nathaniel asked me, his tone low, dangerously even. "She would make me hunt you down. She would make the League, all the angels who consider you a friend hunt you down. There would be no concessions. There would be no more training with Adriel, no hanging with Dev and V. She would make us hurt you, Raven."

There was this tremble in his voice that had me walking round to face him and I placed my hands on my hips. Nathaniel's black eyes bore a hole in me, his handsome face wearing the mask he liked to don when he was trying to keep his emotions in check.

"I was messing, Nate. C'mon. Think logically on it... I'm fast but I can't outrun an angel in flight. Ya, I might get lucky and find some trees for cover, but you'd find me. If I thought I had a chance of getting away, you know I'd take it in a heartbeat, but we both know I can't so what's the point in wasting my energy?"

"The fact that you have obviously gone through all the possible scenarios already does nothing to comfort me."

I laughed, then turned to walk away. "Hey, it's not my fault if you can't handle the truth. Yes, I thought about it. No, I'm not going to."

I continue walking down the hill, the rustle of wings the only indication that Nathaniel is following me. He falls into step beside me, a slight brush of his wing against my back and I shivered. The little touches, the teasing grazes, they all felt intentional, like he was trying to desensitize me to the intimate touches, and they made me unsure of myself.

Nathaniel was a complication, one that made me lose focus. I'd meant to unravel the bonds of the angels one by one, but instead, the circumstances of the last few weeks had only seemed to make them stronger, and that included the bonds I shared with them. But with Nathaniel, there was a chance that more than bones could be broken.

"Where are we going now?" I asked him, shivering

when a blast of wind came out of nowhere and I shuddered.

"Are you cold?"

Shrugging, I pulled the sleeves of my hoodie down over my hands. "A little. But I can handle a little cold."

The night had seeped in around us, and Nathaniel's wings seemed to blend in with the darkness, and for a moment, we looked like two humans out for a stroll in the black of night. I heard a shriek from the distance, then the sound of a gunshot and I froze, wondering how close the Rebels might be.

"What were you like as a child? As a teenager?" Nathaniel queried and I snorted.

"You know what my childhood was like, Nathaniel."

"I didn't ask you what your childhood was like, Raven." Nathaniel said, using the strength of his wing to nudge me into motion again. "I wanted to know who you were."

Mulling over Nathaniel's question, I tugged on the strings of my hoodie before I replied. "Lonely. A lot of the time I was lonely. Because of my power, the other kids were scared of me, and my mother liked it like that. The friends I have now, they were all older so they were already on missions and shit when I was younger."

"That must have been hard."

"It helped me deal with being down in the abyss for three years."

Nathaniel didn't respond to that, not that he needed to, considering he was well aware of how long I was down there. I was used to being alone with my own thoughts, whether it was in the barracks or in a prison cell.

"It also made me grateful for the people who cared for me, who weren't afraid of me. So, there is that. I was curious about everything. I wanted to be the best at everything. I trained harder than anyone else, because I didn't want to rely on my power. I might have been the youngest member of my team but I earned my spot."

"There's that stubborn streak." Nathaniel teased, and I shoved him away with a laugh.

"Ya, image that tenfold in a teenager. I gave Tie- I gave my leader so many headaches. I went through this whole phase of not obeying orders."

Nathaniel chuckled, but didn't say anything. However, I could hear the agreement in his tone that I hadn't grown out of that phase...

"You wouldn't have even looked at me back then." It was the truth because while I was preparing to kill the Imperium, I had spent some time in the citadel, learning the layout, the escape routes, the shift patterns. Molly hadn't yet taken over the running of the kitchens so that was why we had never met before. I was so small and fast that it had been easy for me to sneak about.

I swallowed hard, then started. "I saw you once, from a distance. You were sitting on one of the tower windows gazing up at the sky and then you shoved off, and I couldn't breathe. I rushed to the window and then you shot up into the sky, nothing but obsidian in the sky."

Nathaniel frowned. "You were in the citadel that long?"

"As I said." I told him with a lift of my shoulders. "You wouldn't have noticed me then. I was this short, muscular teen with no boobs or curves. They came the following summer and the leaders thought it best for me not to go back to the citadel in case I attracted unwanted attention and put my mission in jeopardy. My sole goal was to get close enough to the Imperium to hill her."

A rustle sounded from the bushes and I yank out my axe, almost laughing when I see a deer galloping out of the forest. It takes one look at me and Nathaniel, looks disgusted at our presence and then loops off again. I sheath my axe again, before elbowing Nathaniel.

"What were you like as a teen angel? Is that a thing? How old does an angel need to be to be considered a baby?"

A chortle of laughter before Nathaniel said. "Time for an angel moves slower, a human year is like a hundred to us. Our babies are normally babies until they reach their two hundredth year. It is acceptable to not be considered an adult until you are a millennia old."

"Jesus Christ...how damn old are you?"

"No. That is something I will not share with you. It makes no difference. I am immortal. The number of years that I have been alive are inconsequential."

I rolled my eyes at his statement, but kept my opinions to myself. I wanted to know more. The slivers of the real Nathaniel from his journals, from the story Verena told me, they all made me hungry to know more about him...from the source itself.

"I too was a curious child, even more so as a young

adult. Mother had always been as she was, the gift of motherhood did not alter her in the slightest. My father however, was the opposite of my mother. He was kind, warm, understanding. A born leader. He treated his inner circle like family, and his League as if they were all his children."

"There are very few leaders like that."

"Indeed." Nathaniel replied, lifting his hand up to run it through his hair. "I wanted to be just like him. He was the angel I aspired to be. Who we all aspired to be. Peace and harmony reigned over the lands with his rule, until my mother grew too impatient and invoked one of our most ancient rites to challenge him."

I didn't want to interrupt him, not when Nathaniel was being so open about his past, and I was learning more about Rieka too, however I found I was more eager to listen to the story, than glean any strategic knowledge from him. That was just a bonus.

"As the son of the Imperium and the son of a member of the League of Dominious, I was held to a certain standard. A reverence. Like a crown prince. The ones who were actively trying to be my friends, were those who hoped to befriend me in the hopes of climbing the social ladder, and the ones who actively scoffed in my presence did not like that two powerful angels had created another one in their mirror."

We reached the outskirts of a village, another once thriving Irish town reduced to rubble and death by the angels. I closed my eyes, wishing that I had known the cities and towns before they had fallen victim to a war that we had never wanted.

I recognised the area, had been here previously to hunt for supplies. The entire town of what used to be Ardee, County Louth, once a beautiful tourist destination, was decimated by death and destruction. Our boots thumped against the broken concrete as we made our way through the town, coming to a halt outside a school. Like the church, its windows were shattered and a wall on one side had been completely blown out, like an explosive had been used.

Nathaniel offered me his hand as I made to climb over the knocked down wall, rolling my eyes as I quickly clambered up and over, dropping into a crouch as Nathaniel flew up and over, landing with a grace as I straightened.

"Show off." I mumbled as I walked toward the building, and Nathaniel only chuckled at me.

Pushing open the door, I had to put some effort into it, the door sticking, before it opened with a loud groan that echoed out through the abandoned school. The darkness seemed endless, as the wind howled through, as Nathaniel came in behind me, folding his wings in tight in the narrow space.

"What was your father like?" Nathaniel asked me suddenly and I forgot to school my expression.

Oh, nothing to boast about, really. He was a scumbag angel who took my mother by force and she got me as a constant reminder of the worst time in her life. If I ever find him, I'll kill him...

"I have no clue," I admitted, hoping it would cover my expression. "I never met him and my mother doesn't talk about him."

"I'm sorry, Raven."

I waved off Nathaniel's pity. "Don't be. It is what it is. I have no desire to know who he is or was. He just gave me parts of my DNA, that's it and all I need to know."

Glass crunches under my boot as I walk down the hallway. "How do we know that there aren't any rabid creatures ready to pounce on us and eat us alive?"

"The only heartbeats I can hear are our own."

I spin round, putting my hands on the wall to stop Nathaniel from slipping by me. "You can hear my heartbeat? Can you hear it all the time?"

A slight smirk tugged at the corners of his mouth. "Not consciously. Angelic hearing is better than a human's, as are all our other senses. But as everything is louder, I have to focus to be able to drown out other sounds. In this quiet, yes, I can hear your heart beat."

The damn organ started to pick up pace then as Nathaniel's smile deepened. "Does that worry you, Raven?"

I let my hands fall to my sides. Of course it fucking worried me. I was suddenly only thinking about how much my heart rate kicked up when Nathaniel touched me, when he stopped being a dickhead and pretended to be nice and I fell for it. My pulse jumped as my lips parted and he dipped his head so that if either of us edged forward just a tad, our lips could crash together.

"Like now, your heart is racing. What just ran through that brain of yours?"

I licked my lips, noting how his eyes tracked the movement. "I was thinking that it's gonna be terrible if an angel can tell how excited I get before I make them bleed. That's all."

His expression told me that he was calling bullshit on my answer but whatever.

Just when I thought he might call my bluff, he stiffened. "We are no longer alone."

That was the only warning I got before something barrelled into me, knocking me into the small classroom. I landed on my side, rolled onto my back, scrambling back as a wastelander shrieked at me from the doorway. It appeared male, about five foot ten in height, not that you could tell by the way its body was contorted. You could see the bite marks in its own flesh where it had either gnawed on itself or had been eaten by another wastelander. Bones protruded from its sickly pale skin, cracked and blistered as it was.

It took in some air, its chest sort of inflating and deflating as the thing shrieked at me again. I heard Nathaniel call my name. I ignored him, as the waste-lander, opened its mouth, its jagged yellow and black teeth flashing before it lunged for me, jaws snapping.

I rolled to the side, got to my feet and had my axe in my hand between one breath and the next. I didn't want to throw it and miss, leaving me with no weapon. I feigned a move to the left, the creature lunging that way, and I grabbed for it, avoiding its attempt to have a munch on me.

Nathaniel was having difficulty getting in through the smaller doors, his wings getting stuck and he couldn't risk throwing a fireball and hitting me by mistake so I was on my own. No big deal. I'd killed enough wasterlanders to know what I was doing, even if I was a little rusty.

Bending my leg I hooked my heel to kick the thing at the back of its knees and it shrieked at me again as I hoisted up my axe and chopped down. The thing convulsed in my arms as I let go of it, then I slashed down again, separating his head from his shoulders. It was unnerving to watch as the body twitched once before laying still.

I tossed the head toward the back of the classroom, then headed out as I looked for something to clean the gore off my axe before I put it away. Nathaniel looked furious, though I wasn't sure why, until he snarled. "I was useless to you."

I was amused that he had felt useless during the fight but it wasn't like I needed him. Glancing down at his black t-shirt, I pulled it out of the waistband of his cargos, ignoring the sharp intake of breath as I wiped the blade with the fabric and then let it fall back in place.

"See, there. You were useful. Happy now?"

His scowl told me that he was not.

"Can we get this meeting over with yet? I'm starving."

Nathaniel put his hand on my shoulder when I made

to walk down the corridor, handed me a little package. I unwrapped it, found some of the chocolate bites that both me and Grainger liked, popped one into my mouth and then begrudgingly, offered one to Nathaniel.

"I'm good."

"More for me then. Cheers."

Nathaniel rolled his eyes, then pointed down the hall. "Head for the gymnasium. We will meet my contact there."

I followed his instructions, heading down the hallway, keeping an ear out in case any more things wanted to jump out of darkened rooms to try and have me for dinner. When nothing did, I finished my chocolate, then said. "I always wanted to go to a school like this. Well, not like this exactly but you know what I mean."

"Did you not go to school?"

I peered over my shoulder at Nathaniel as I reached out and traced my fingers over a faded painting of the map of the world. "I did, but you know it's not normal school when you have firearms training between history and lunch. I guess knowing random things about rocks or maths, doesn't matter as much when your life is on the line."

We reach the end of the hall, and the gymnasium and Nathaniel steps passed me to glance inside before pushing down on the handle and opening both doors. I wandered inside, looking around. The hall was empty apart from some rubbish floating around in the gusty wind. Benches were rotted on either side and two chipped basketball rims on either side. One of the rims is bent like someone tried to hang onto it.

Scanning the room, I spot a basketball in the corner and jog over to get it. Amazingly, it's only a little flat. I bounce it once, twice, then walk over and stand under the net and take a shot. The ball goes through the hoop and I grinned.

Nathaniel stood off to the side. Leaning against the wall he watched me as I dribbled the ball between my legs in a figure eight, and then grasped it in my hands before I aimed again, giving a little whoop of laughter as it went through with ease.

I kicked up the ball, turning it over in my hands, as air came out through a pinprick in the ball. Looking over at Nathaniel, I lifted my brows. "You wanna loan me some of the hot air in ya to help me pump up the ball. I'm sure you've got loads to spare."

Nathaniel shot me an unamused glare as I heard laughter coming from the far end of the hall that had me dropping the ball and kept my feet firmly rooted to the spot.

"Hello Trouble."

I whirled round, my heart wanting to jump out of my chest with joy. I allowed myself a minute to bask in it, in the sight of him standing in the same room as me. He looks older, his ginger hair still as bright as I remember, his smile still as warm and inviting as the twinkle of mischief in his eyes. He grinned at me, taking a step toward me and I wanted to run and throw my arms around his neck.

My mind was riddled with too much to think clearly and all too soon the joy was iced over by fear and all I knew is that I had to protect Tiernan from Nathaniel.

Unlatching my axe, I took off at a run, throwing the axe in Nathaniel's direction. I knew it wouldn't wound him, but I had to distract him from the person I cared about most in this world, and get him to safety.

I glanced over as Nathaniel snapped out his hand and caught the axe, blade first in his palm, reminding me of the time I had hurled the axe aiming for Saskia. I heard him grunt, ignored it as I came up to Tiernan who was watching me with an amused expression.

Shoving at his shoulders, I growled. "You need to leave right this fucking minute Tiernan Byrne or so help me I will drag you out by your foxy head!"

Tiernan burst out laughing. "Jaysus, Raven. I've fucking missed you."

I pushed him again. "Stop that. Turn around and walk out the damn door right now. Please, Tiernan. GO!"

Tiernan reached out and placed his hands on my shoulders. "Raven, it's okay. The commander won't hurt me."

Then Tiernan wrapped his arms around my shoulders and pulled me into a hug. I wrapped my arms around his waist, breathing in the scent of him, and it felt like home. My heart was pounding inside my chest as we stood in the gymnasium and I didn't want to let him go just in case this was a figment of my imagination.

I felt Tiernan kiss the top of my head, then he patted my back. "I know that the commander won't kill me but from the way he's looking at me now, Trouble, if you hold me any tighter, he might reconsider hurting me."

Laughing, I reluctantly stepped back from Tiernan's warmth and swiped the wetness from my eyes. "Ew, I love you, Tiernan but even if I was your type, you're my brother."

Tiernan reached out and ruffled my hair. "Right back at ya, little sister. Now go apologize for making him bleed before he takes back safe passage."

"He'll get over it. He always does."

Nathaniel chuckled as he strode over, holding the axe out to me. "That wasn't very nice now, was it?"

"Neither was keeping the fact that we were meeting Tiernan from me." I snatched the axe back and sheathed it.

"I didn't disclose who we were meeting on the off chance that Tiernan wasn't able to get away to meet us. I did not want you to be disappointed."

Well, now I felt like a right bitch.

I scowled, which made Tiernan laugh, and I glared at him and he held up his hands. "I know that face anywhere. It's your I know I should say sorry but I'm too stubborn to."

"Fuck off, Tiernan. Fuck right off."

Tiernan was still smiling as he held out his hand to Nathaniel. "Commander."

"Tiernan."

The familiarity between them made me suspicious as I folded my arms across my chest. "So, who wants to be the one to tell me exactly how you two seem to be best buddies."

Tiernan reached out and patted my cheek, and I swatted his hand away. "Stop that and spill already."

Glancing at Nathaniel, Tiernan waited until Nathaniel gave a slight incline of his head before Tiernan began to speak and the fact that Tiernan had to wait for Nathaniel's permission before speaking grated on me more than I would ever admit.

"A year after the attempt on the Imperium, we lost a

whole squad of soldiers to the Seraphan. I didn't know who they were at the time, but I was caught up in it. I had a stomach wound that should have killed me, but then the commander had shown up and he had some angel heal me, kept me alive until I was strong enough to walk back home."

I looked at Nathaniel. "Did you know who he was when you helped him? What angle were you working when you had Adair heal him?"

Nathaniel lowered his lashes for a moment, like he was exasperated that I would accuse him of working any sort of angle. "There was no angle. Tiernan kept Takara at bay when he could have killed Adair, distracted him from his killing blow. Adair healed him and while he was resting, I made Tiernan an offer."

It was my turn to look at Tiernan then, my friend just grinning. "So, you go around saving angels now?"

"Just the hot ones." Tiernan remarked with a wink and I rolled my eyes, motioning for Tiernan to continue.

"We made a bargain, the commander and me." Tiernan explained to me, his smile not faltering once. "He would divert the scouts in areas the Rebels were looking for supplies, after leaving supplies for us to find, and in turn I would trade him information that wouldn't cause harm to the Rebels."

"You sold us out."

"I put food on the fucking table, Raven. I kept my soldiers alive. I gave him little details, and he knows it. I got the better half of the deal. And when rumours started to reach us about a human with the power to go invisible was strutting round the citadel, I finally had the courage to ask the commander if you were alive."

I felt shitty for accusing him when I had been making friends with the angels myself. I had no right to judge Tiernan for what he had done to stay alive, just as he had no right to judge me for what I'd had to do to stay alive.

"I'm sorry," I ground out, Tiernan's brows lifting and even Nathaniel's mouth twitched. "And that is probably the only time you will ever hear that coming out of my mouth so commit it to memory."

The two males laughed, and I rolled my eyes. Tiernan reached out and touched my arm.

"I had been meeting with the commander for months and I couldn't risk asking him about you in case you were dead or worse. When he confirmed that you were indeed alive, and still being the Trouble I know and love, I was ready to storm the citadel with James to get you back."

"Well, that would have been stupid, considering your face and James's mug are two of the most recognisable faces of the Rebels."

Tiernan winked, his blue eyes twinkling. "The penance for being handsome bastards, I suppose."

That made me laugh, the sound seemingly surprising Nathaniel because he was looking at me like he'd never heard me laugh before.

"Speaking of supplies," Nathaniel interrupted, rolling his shoulders and his wings shifted to brush my arm again and Tiernan watched the gesture with amusement. "Did you get the supplies I dropped at the check-point last week?"

Tiernan nodded his head. "We did, thanks. We've had a bad dose of flu the last couple weeks so the medicine is greatly appreciated."

"Leave me a list at the same place the next time you're running low. I'll try and get my hands on anything I can."

My eyes darted back and forth. This was fucking surreal, right? A Rebel and an angel having a polite conversation about helping one another like it was normal for them to be standing here, together, and chatting away like our two peoples weren't at war.

My mouth opened, then closed, and then opened again. A growl of frustration came out and I stalked away, muttering to myself as I heard Tiernan say. "I think we broke her."

"The quiet is a nice change of pace."

I gave them both the finger as I walked over to the half-rotted stands and sat my ass down on one after I tested it to make sure I wouldn't fall through it. I rested my elbows on my knees, my chin in my hands as I tried to come to terms with the fact that Nathaniel, the son of the most hated angel in all of Ireland, was actively helping to keep the Rebels alive.

What the actual fuck?

"I need for you to understand that I am not a monster and that the things I do, are to protect those I care for. Even if doing some of it kills a part of me with the consequences."

It made me wonder would Nathaniel have even

brought me out here to see Tiernan if he hadn't wanted me to be less afraid of him. I understood that he had shown me just how much I didn't know about the inner workings of the League, of what he was doing, because while I despised what he had done to Adriel with Raisel, I couldn't be mad at him for keeping Tiernan safe.

Tiernan said something to Nathaniel and he nodded, going back out the double doors as Tiernan came over to where I was sat and nudged me with his shoulder. "Still happy to see me?"

Snarling, I punched his shoulder. "You know I am. Out of everyone, I missed you the most. Just don't tell James."

"I promise." Tiernan said with a laugh, looking over to the spot Nathaniel had vacated. "He cares about you."

I made a noncommittal sound, leaning my head against Tiernan's shoulder, closing my eyes.

"You always had trouble letting people in."

"Never you," I told Tiernan with a sigh. "You are the only one who managed to win me over so quickly. Even James had to work hard at it."

"I'm special." Tiernan teased, then he took my hand in his, gave it a little squeeze. "You will never know just how happy I felt when I heard you backchatting to the commander like you used to do with me. I worried that the things you'd been through might have broken your spirit. It only seems to have made you stronger."

"Your trauma has made you stronger."

Adriel had said that to me not too long ago and now it felt like Tiernan was saying it to me too. I wanted to tell him the same thing I had told Adriel, however, Tiernan had to walk away tonight from me and I had to go back into the citadel. In order to ensure that he worried less after seeing me intact, I would leave him to the illusion that I wasn't a wreck on the inside.

"So, you think Adair is handsome?"

Tiernan grinned, the mischief in his eyes dancing. "Do you think the commander is handsome?"

A flush heated my cheeks as Tiernan grinned, as I ignored his question. "You know Adair has a twin...an identical twin..."

I let my voice trail off as I wiggled my eyebrows and Tiernan bumped his shoulder to mine. "Two of them. Huh...and identical...that could be fun...I'd ask for an introduction but we don't tend to hang out in the same circles."

"If I get the chance, I'll put in a good word with Adair for you. His twin not so much. Adriel is more like me."

Tiernan reached over and tugged on my braid. "You're fond of him, this Adriel."

"I know I shouldn't be but I am. It didn't start out that way and it will probably be the death of me in the end, but I think of him as a brother."

"As someone you call brother on a regular basis, that is high praise indeed."

The double doors opened and Nathaniel came back in. From the look on his face, it was time to leave and I didn't want to go back. I wanted to go home with Tiernan. I wanted to see James. It was harder now to go back after seeing Tiernan in the flesh after so long.

I stayed rooted to the spot, unable to be the first to make the move to break up the reunion, and I was surprised to see Nathaniel simply lean on the wall again, giving me time to say goodbye to Tiernan. Who knew when I would see him again...if I would...

Tiernan got to his feet, still holding onto my hand, then he dragged me up into a hug. The minutes ticked by as I clung to him, not wanting to say goodbye. The last time we had said goodbye, I was walking into what we had suspected would be the death of me.

My fingers dug into his back, holding him close, and it was Tiernan who had to untangle himself from my grasp. He brushed a thumb over my cheek and then I realized I was crying.

"Hey, no tears now, Trouble. This isn't goodbye. It's not like last time."

"How did you know that's what I was thinking about?"

Tiernan cupped my cheek, pressed a kiss to my forehead before he said. "You had the same look on your face then as you do now. I love ya, Trouble. Don't forget that. I'll see you soon."

He walked away from me then, as my heart felt like it was going to shatter into a million little pieces. I watched as Tiernan and Nathaniel shook hands, with Tiernan saying something to Nathaniel, the angel glancing at me before he inclined his head to Tiernan.

The man I loved like a brother was almost to the door he had come in through when I shouted. "Tiernan!"

With a massive grin, Tiernan turned back to look at me as I said. "I love you too."

He winked at me one last time before he was gone and I stood there like an idiot, silent tears streaming down my face. My vision blurred as I tried to stop myself from completely losing my shit.

Strong arms wrapped around me, pulling me into a wall of muscle and I felt too raw to push him away. Like I had with Tiernan, I wrapped my arms around his waist and just held him, letting Nathaniel trace circles around my spine and pretended that this changed nothing between us.

When I finally ran out of tears, I stepped back from Nathaniel, looking up into his onyx-coloured eyes. "Thank you." My voice sounded hoarse, so I cleared it and tried again, but Nathaniel got there before me.

"Had I known that seeing Tiernan would make you so sad, then I might have reconsidered making you aware of our alliance."

"I am sad," I told him, swiping at my eyes again. "But I'm also happy to see him. I wouldn't trade the moment of pure joy of seeing him in the flesh again over the heartbreak of being separated from him again for anything. So, thank you. And thank you for making sure he was alive for me to see again. I can't thank Adair though, can I?"

Nathaniel shook his head. "No. Not yet. The only ones who will know what happened this night are you, me, Tiernan, and Raisel. Some secrets must be kept in order to keep those we care for safe."

Fuck. I hated to admit it, but Nathaniel was right. In order to keep Tiernan safe, I couldn't tell anyone Nathaniel had made it happen because it would put Nathaniel *and* Tiernan in danger. And as much as I wanted to be honest with Adriel, in order to keep him safe, keep him sane even, I couldn't tell him about Raisel, or Nathaniel's part in it all.

I was quiet on the walk back and Nathaniel didn't try and get me to talk at all. He even waited while I inhaled the fresh air outside the door we had left through this morning, and when I lingered just a little too long, he held open the door and said. "Come inside, Raven. Let's get you a cup of that tea you like to warm you up."

Knowing I couldn't stay outside too much longer, I ducked under Nathaniel's arm and shook off the cold. We walked down the corridor, heading back to the League quarters. I went to head into the kitchen, thinking Nathaniel would try and come in with me, but he paused in the hall.

"You want some tea?" I asked him and I could see he looked torn.

"I must inform the Imperium that we have returned in person. Go have your tea and I will see you tomorrow."

Of course he'd have to go and tell the bitch we were back. It clawed away some of the good grace Nathaniel taking me to see Tiernan had gotten him, even if I knew that it had to have cost him something to ask his mother for a favour.

"Okay. And again, thank you. I won't forget this, Nate."

Nathaniel studied me for a hard minute, and I don't know what was running through his head but it heated the blood in my veins far quicker than the tea ever could. The look on his face, was the look of a man who was at war with himself and it seared through me, making me fight the urge to slide my hands into his hair and yank his head down for a kiss.

"Raven." My name sounded pained as it passed through his lips, then he snapped into movement, coming over to cup my face in his hands. "I want so badly to kiss you. But not when you feel like you owe me something. No. When I kiss you, and I will, it will be because this thread between us too much for us to deny and then, I will sate myself with this maddening need I have for you."

Nathaniel is gone before I can even process his words, leaving me breathless in the hall as I glance from side to side, into the horrified face of Hayes, who just shook his head before he too left me standing in the hall, with no clue as to what the fuck just happened.

CHAPTER
SEVENTEEN

After a fitful sleep, I woke to a note from Nathaniel left on my bedside table to advise me that he had cancelled my training with Adriel to allow me to rest up after yesterday. At first, I was pissed as hell thinking that Nathaniel had cancelled my training because he was fearful that I would tell Adriel about Raisel.

I wanted to dammit, I really did...but I knew deep down that I couldn't.

Nathaniel's note, in the elegant handwriting of his, also told me that he would see me at dinner. The thought of sitting around the dinner table with all the angels and lying my ass off didn't exactly feel like a great way to spend my time.

I spent the day alternating from pacing my room, to trying to read some of my book, then moving furniture in the room because I was so restless. When Verena came to knock on my door to go to dinner, I told her that I wasn't feeling well and just wanted to try and sleep it off. She had asked me if something had happened, and I had shaken my head, telling her no, that I just felt a little under the weather.

It was the same excuse I gave to Devika the next morning when I asked her to tell Adriel that I wouldn't be at training that morning as I still felt unwell. And like the coward I was, when he came to knock for dinner later that night, I pretended to be asleep, my eyes slammed shut.

I knew I couldn't keep pretending to be sick, and Nathaniel would soon come to see what was wrong with me, but I suspected that he already knew why I was avoiding everyone. If he thought I was just being obstinate, then he'd have come to drag my ass to training or dinner, but he let me be. For the first time since we had met, Nathaniel was giving me space to deal with things my way.

"I want so badly to kiss you. But not when you feel like you owe me something. No. When I kiss you, and I will, it will be because this thread between us too much for us to deny and then, I will sate myself with this maddening need I have for you."

That had been his declaration, a promise of what to expect if I allowed us to barrel down that path. I wanted to know what it would be like to feel my body melt at someone's touch and not be left feeling cold in my bones. Nathaniel only had to look at me and I craved him. It would consume us, in the end, because one night would never be enough for Nathaniel, and I still was actively planning on killing his mother.

And then there had been Hayes.

That look in his eyes as my gaze had found his told me that he had seen the entire interaction between me and Nathaniel. His face had been complete and utter disgust, horror, and he had dismissed me with a shake of his head. His expression told me that in his head, I had betrayed him, and I knew that it hadn't even crossed his mind that it might be a betrayal to the Rebels.

It was my own fault really. One of the biggest regrets I had was allowing myself to breach the line between friend and lover with Hayes, knowing I didn't return his feelings. At the time I believed I was incapable of feeling the same way about Hayes as he did for me, because something was lacking in me. Instead, I was attracted to a cocky angel who got on my nerves one minute and surprised me the next.

Hayes had obviously thought our fumble meant more than it did, my quick exit once he was finished not seeming to deter him. I remembered avoiding him for the next couple of days, claiming to prepare for going to the citadel, but the night before I left, as I walked out of my final meeting with the elders, Hayes had cornered me.

I walked out of the room and almost collided with Hayes. Shame flooded through me at the change in the way his eyes looked at me now. Before, I had been able to ignore the way his eyes roamed over me, with a longing that was as clear as a pane of glass. Now though, there was the look of intimacy in his gaze as he reached out to touch my arm and I side stepped it.

"Raven, what's going on?"

197

"*You know what's going on, Hayes. I'm going to the citadel tomorrow and will probably lose my head.*"

Hayes paled, attempting to reach for me again, and I snarled, talking off down the hall. I heard him swear, then follow me and I wanted to pull my power around me and just avoid this brutal awkwardness between us now. It had been my fault. I was the one who snuck into his room that night. I had been the one to take off all my clothes as his eyes watched with a sort of reverence. It was me who climbed into his bed, kissed him and tried to warm the coldness in me with his body.

I had used Hayes, used his attraction to me, and I had fucking ruined the years of friendship because I hadn't wanted to go to my death without knowing what it was like to get hot and sweaty between the sheets...not that I had gotten hot or sweaty...

"*That's not what I meant and you know it. I know that you are scared of what happens tomorrow, but I'll be right there with you.*"

I whirled round, a vicious growl in my throat. "*No. No Hayes, you won't be right there with me. I'll be alone. I'm the one that everyone is depending on to kill the Imperium and not you. Me.*"

I stabbed at my chest, slapping Hayes' hand away when he reached for me a third time. "*Don't fucking touch me.*"

"*Why are you being like this? I just want to hold you. This might be the last night we get to spend together, Raven. God, the other night was the best night of my life and you won't even let me hold you?*"

His words grated on me and I wanted to cringe at how

pathetic he sounded. I should tell him that right this minute, shatter the illusion that he had about me. But I had hurt him and that would just be like twisting the dagger inside his heart.

Tomorrow I would probably be dead and I'd never have to worry about Hayes and his unrequited feelings for me. It almost made me laugh to think that death was easier than having to deal with Hayes and his puppy dog eyes.

I didn't say anything, just stood there with a mask of indifference on my face. I remembered the feel of his hands on me as they caressed my body, the chill that seemed to spread from my heart to the rest of my body, the way my body had tensed the moment he was inside me, and how I had laid there, staring at the ceiling until it was over. I had never felt so hollow.

I wanted to erase that handful of moments from my memories.

"Raven, I know you must be scared of what will happen after but..."

"Ugh," I ground out, shaking my head. "I'm not scared of what comes after, Hayes. I'm numb to it all. I don't care what happens to me after, once the Imperium is dead. Don't you get that? I know my life was never meant to be long, right? We Rebels don't die of old age, Hayes. We die bloody on the battlefield. This is the culmination of everything I have trained for."

"Don't talk like that, Raven. I can't stand it."

He couldn't stand it? Like I had the time to care about what he could or could not stand.

I needed to get away from him before I said something that I regretted.

If I died, then after I had treated him so badly, I owed him the false memories that we both considered that night something special.

Or maybe I really was just a coward who didn't want to break his heart.

Turning away from Hayes, I sighed. "If I fail..."

Hayes grabbed my arm, spinning me around. "You won't fail, Raven. I won't leave you behind. I'll come looking for you no matter what the elders say. We don't leave each other behind."

Hayes pressed his lips to mine, his grip on me tightening and yet, I couldn't bring myself to respond because I didn't feel the way Hayes felt about me. I couldn't.

Because I could never truly be myself with him...with anyone.

Hayes pulled back, determination in his voice as he said. "Until I see your body, I will always wait for you to come home. I will always wait."

A knock sounded on my door and dragged me from my memories. I swallowed down the sicky feeling in my throat and called out for whoever it was to come in, bracing myself with a mask guarding my expression for whoever came in.

I was surprised that it was Adair who walked in.

"Hey Raven."

His smile was warm, his bright green eyes always a stark reminder of how much the light had been diminished in his twin's eyes after everything that had been done to him. Adair came over to the bed, waiting until I told him to have a seat before he folded his legs under him and perched on the end of the bed. His black and green wings were pulled tight against his back as he ran his gaze over me.

"Adriel was worried that you were unwell. He asked me to check on you to make sure that it wasn't something I could help with."

I felt so fucking ashamed that I had to look away. "I'm grand. It's just a very human few days of feeling blah and I'm already starting to feel a little better. Adriel worries too much."

Adair ran a hand through his unruly hair. "It was how he was before he was taken. After, it was as if the pain of others suffering didn't so much as flicker with the healer he used to be. It is in our nature to heal, compulsively so. It was why I had been under the falsehood that when I was healing you at the start, that I was helping you."

Heart clenching at the reminder, I shifted my gaze back to Adair. "We squared that away. I mean, I'm keeping you on your toes with how much I get injured, and most of it I ask to be done to me so we are all good."

That seemed to appease Adair, and I was surprised at how much I meant it. I would never forget what had been done to me, what Adair had helped do to me, but Adair had also saved the person I loved most in this fucked up world and though I couldn't thank him outright, letting go of my discourse with him was the least I could do.

"I must confess," Adair mused with a small smile. "That it gave me hope to see Adriel worry that you were unwell, because it showed that he is starting to find a new way to be. We sat down long after the others had gone to bed the other night and just spoke for hours, like we used to. He is not the same as before, and I accept that, but I think my brother is finally coming home."

I pulled my knees to my chest. "I'm glad. And I'm glad he decided to take a room down the hall again. Being alone can be very addictive to a person who has to fight against their monsters every day."

Cocking his head to the side, Adair studied me for a moment. "You sometimes speak with the wisdom of age that it shocks me when I remember that you are barely born."

It wasn't an insult really, because to an angel, I was barely born.

With a shrug of my shoulders, I rested my chin on my knee, then chuckled. "I don't think if you asked many people they would call me wise. Reckless, stubborn, prone to angry outbursts, and with a severe allergic reaction to authority. That about sums me up."

"I do think," Adair said after taking a minute to mull over my words. "That you sell yourself short a lot. I have spent a lot of time trying to figure you out and I still can't. However, I do believe that you have forgotten a few adjectives. Brave, selfless, kind, courageous, to name but a few. You willingly put yourself in harm's way to protect those you care for, even if it means harming yourself. I think you aren't as kind with yourself as you are with others."

I brushed off his words and my embarrassment with a roll of my eyes. "Stop, Adair or I might think that you are flirting with me."

Adair chuckled, then shook his head. "Perish the thought. And while I meant every single word and you are using that wit of yourself to deflect, I can assure you that though I have some affection for you, it would never be romantic. I am not attracted to females."

Well, that was an interesting slice of information that would make Tiernan happy.

I grinned, then sighed. "I'm the wrong person to come to if you wanted a girlie chat about good looking boys. I'm more likely to get turned on by a sharp blade than a cute guy. I'm not entirely all the way sane."

Adair barked out a laugh. "There is no one quite like you, Raven Cassidy."

"Thank fuck for that! Could you imagine how busy you'd be if there was two of me?"

I was grinning as Adair said. "It might be worth it just to see Nathaniel's feathers ruffled. We are all taking bets on how long before the two of you finally stop with the back and forth and just, what is it the humans like to say, hook up already?"

That made me growl, and Adair just laughed.

"Who the hell started that? Let me guess, Verena?"

Adair crossed a finger over his heart. "I am sworn to secrecy. However, if you would like to share my winnings, and maybe yanking Nathaniel from his sour mood, then I would appreciate if you and he would get naked between then end of this week and next."

"Fucking hell. You guys are ridiculous. I bet Adriel is too mature to get involved in this bullshit."

Adair snickered and I let my mouth fall open. "No fucking way. Adriel, really? He's in on it too?"

With a nod of his head, Adair confirmed that his twin was very much involved in the betting. "Adriel said that you both are as stubborn as the other, and that he suspected that ye quite enjoyed the verbal sparring too much to put an end to it with a tryst in the bedroom. He thinks we can expect more of the same for a time to come. Adriel has always had a very strategic mind, so as much as I hate to say it, I think he might be right."

I let loose a humph of annoyance. "You all need to get laid. For fuck sake."

"So, do you, darling. Next week preferably." Adair said in a dry tone and that made me bark out a laugh.

"Asshole." I muttered as Adair got to his feet, the smile on his face still curving his lips.

"Right, since I came to check on your wellbeing and you seem to be alright, do you fancy a walk?"

Going for a walk meant maybe running into angels I wasn't ready to face yet, and although I was starting to have cabin fever, I needed a little more time. As if he sensed my reluctance, an expression of understanding crossed over his face.

"If you are worried about running into Nathaniel, he is on duty today and won't be back until later tonight. I think you might just be intrigued enough by where I'm going to come with me."

Adair strode over and out the door, hesitating in the hall as I sighed, then got out of bed to slip my feet into my boots and grabbed a jumper before I headed after Adair. After all the shocks I'd gotten over the last few days, I was mentally preparing myself for another slap in the face as I walked beside Adair.

We walked down the hall, past the library and then Adair went to a wall and with a grin, pushed hard on the wall. It swung inward, revealing a passageway that had me instantly curious and committing its location to memory.

"C'mon. I promise this will be worth the secrecy."

I followed Adair into the passageway, the door closing beside us as we walked in silence. I could feel the chill in the air, wondered if Adair was taking me outside as he came to a metal gate and pushed it open, the grey of the day greeting us.

We stepped outside, my feet standing on what seemed to be a viewing platform that overlooked a courtyard not dissimilar to the League's private training ground, but it had a massive drop to get to the stone below. There didn't look like there was any way for someone without wings to get down below, though I know it could be hidden. It was wider, almost the same size as a football pitch. The viewing platform went around in a rectangle, with various gaps to allow for an angel take flight.

I glanced at Adair. "Planning to push me off?"

"No. Look over there, Raven."

On the opposite side of where we stood, I finally notice Devika, her silver hair and grey wings stepping out of the shadows. But it was not Devika that I focused on but the angel beside her. He looked to be no more than ten years old, his wings a rich brown with tips of gold around the edges. He nodded at something Devika said, then I heard myself scream as Devika pushed the angelic child off the ledge and he plummeted toward the ground.

I moved before I could remember that I had no wings to carry me downward, with Adair grabbing me before I too plummeted to the concrete below. I shoved at Adair, horror and revulsion in my face as I watched the boy snap out his wings at the last minute, then glide across the space, before he beat his wings hard enough to rise up higher and higher.

"You really thought that Dev had pushed him off to harm him, didn't you?"

I could hear the bitter disappointment in his tone, as I spared him a glance and shrugged my shoulders. "In my defence, my mother had me electrocuted in order to desensitize me to torture tactics. My default is always the bad rather than the good. I knew that Dev wouldn't hurt him but I still forgot that for a second."

Adair blinked at my honest remark, then looked over to where the young angel had landed beside Devika, who high fived him, then ruffled his hair. The boy beamed, as Devika spoke to him.

"Devika's powers mean she is a good tutor for the young angels. She can stop them from hurting themselves by manipulating the air and suspend them midfall."

Now that Adair pointed it out to me, I could see the logic in it, and Devika was so damn happy all the time, she was a reassuring mentor to have. I glanced around and saw no other angelic children in the vicinity. Why was this child getting individual training by himself and not with his other angels?

I asked Adair this, glancing back at the boy, before Adair said. "He will one day be one of us."

This child was powerful enough to one day become a soldier in the League of Dominious.

It was hard to believe that this angelic child would one day be one of Nathaniel's elite soldiers, and I wondered what power he might possess to have gotten on the League's radar. Devika waved over to us then, and I lifted my hand in greeting.

"Don't tell her I thought she'd pushed him off to die. I don't want to hurt her feelings."

Adair glanced at me, but nodded his head. "Of course. I should have warned you first."

I watched this time as Devika gave the boy a nudge after pointing over to where I stood with Adair, the boy snapping out his wings the moment he was in the air this time, though it still made my stomach somersault.

Devika took flight an instant later, the two angels coming over where we stood.

The boy landed with a grace that I'd seen in most angels, but more so with the League and I could almost feel the power coming from him. With eyes the same colour as his hair and wings, the boy stared at me with wide eyes. His face was covered in freckles, his face missing the harshness that came with a child forced into war too soon, and I was glad for it.

"Who are you?" He asked me, folding his wings in when Devika tapped his shoulders.

"Don't be rude, Zephyr." Devika said in a stern tone but she was smiling.

I grinned at the boy. "Don't worry about it. I like blunt. I'm Raven."

The boy's eyes widened, his mouth parting. "Invisible girl?"

I lifted my eyes to Devika, her silver eyes sparkling as she shrugged. "You are quite infamous in the citadel. Even the young have heard about you."

"Can I see it? Your power?" The boy was almost gleeful with excitement as Adair ruffled his hair.

"Zeph, you have better manners than that."

The boy's shoulders sagged as he said. "I'm sorry. May I see your power please?"

I called my power forth, watched as the boy stepped back with a gasp. "That is so cool. I can't wait to tell my mom that I got to meet Raven too."

Letting go of my power, I returned the boy's grin.

"It's nice to meet you too, Zephyr. I've never met an angel like you before."

Devika reached out and squeezed the boy's shoulder. "You wanna show Raven your power? I think she'd like to see it."

The boy nodded, shifting his gaze to Adair, who smirked, then said. "Raven loves her axe. It should be in her room."

I was puzzled as to why Adair was giving Zephyr all that information when the boy nodded, a look of pure concentration on his face as he held out his right hand and between one blink and the next, my axe was in my hand.

"Fuck me that's a cool power to have."

Adair shook his head, as Zephyr grinned, handing me my axe. "It's a nice axe. Did the commander really give it to you as a present?"

My cheeks heated, though thankfully, Zephyr didn't seem to notice but the other two angels did, and they laughed and I bloody ignored them.

"Man, I wish I had your power. It would be handy to be able to summon anything I want. Is it only weapons or can you like summon chocolate to eat with all your friends?"

In answer to my question, the boy grinned, held out his left hand and then he was holding a few of those chocolate bites that I always ate in his hands. He handed one to me and I popped it into my mouth, chewing and swallowing before I held up hand, and Zephyr high fived me.

"I wish I had your power. It would be the best way to sneak up on people."

"It is." I agreed, folding my arms across my chest. "Though the commander has some weird superpower that means he can see me even when I go invisible. Don't tell him but it annoys the hell out of me."

Zephyr's eyes widened. "The commander can see you even when you use your power?"

"Yup. Makes me want to punch him."

The boy looked stricken that I would even want to punch Nathaniel and Adair made to speak, but I caught his eye, before I looked at Zephyr again. "I only punch him when we are sparring. But I lose my temper sometimes and while I might want to hit him, I wouldn't."

Zephyr nodded, his shoulders shifting, his wings tipping the floor before he replied. "I get angry sometimes too. My mam tells me that I need to learn to control my anger so it doesn't control me. That a warrior must stay calm in battle. I try, but sometimes I want to punch someone too."

"Your mam sounds like a smart woman." I replied, careful to make sure that I heard him right when he spoke of his mother in the present tense.

"She is a fierce warrior with the League of Dominious and it is my path to one day stand beside her against the Seraphan."

Wait...Zephyr's mother was a member of the League. Jesus Christ, don't tell me that this sweet, innocent child belonged to Saskia because then I would hurl.

"Speaking of your mam," Adair said, as if he had

heard my silent question. "Makata will be back in an hour or so and she wants to run through some drills with you. Why don't you grab a snack, and she'll come get you when she flies in."

The boy looked disappointed, looking to Raven, like he wanted to spend more time with her.

"You need to eat to have lots of energy. Tell ya what. You do what Adair suggested and the next time I see the commander, I'll ask him if I can come see you again. Maybe we can spar a little, if your mam and the commander are okay with that?"

"You'd really want to spend time with me?"

Zephyr sounded so shocked that I would, and I heard the hint of excitement as I reached over and ruffled his hair. "Absolutely. I'd much prefer to spend my time with you than the commander." I told him with a wink, that had him laughing, the sound free and airy before he let Devika take him away, and when he turned to look over his shoulder to give me a bright smile, I returned it.

"How old is he?" I asked Adair as we stood alone now.

"In human terms, Zeph is around eleven years old. In angelic terms, he is decades older."

I wasn't surprised to learn this, because I already knew that angels aged at a different rate than humans. What surprised me was that Zephyr had been born on the other side of the door into our world, that Makata had given birth to him over there and somehow he had ended up here with her.

"I see you have questions, but after seeing the chocolates, now I'm hungry. Shall we go raid the kitchen and then I will answer all the questions you have."

I nodded in agreement, then let Adair lead me back the way we came. We ducked into the kitchen, armed ourselves with enough treats to put us in a food coma, and I grabbed a warm tea before we went into the study. Someone had already lit the fire, and I went straight over to it, lowering myself to the ground, stretching out my legs as I leaned against the side of one of the chairs, setting my axe down on the table in front of me. Adair lowered himself into one of the angel designed chairs, and I ate my weight in junk food and drank my tea before I began to throw questions at Adair.

"How did Zephyr end up over here? It's not like he was old enough to fight and I bet Makata wanted to keep him safe."

Adair slid down in his chair, setting his feet on the coffee table. "Zephyr's father was killed on the other side defending the children. He wasn't a member of the League. No Linden was a teacher of the young, a gentle male who was not built to fight and yet, gave his life to keep the children in his care safe."

That was awful. Heartbreakingly so, but even I knew that Zephyr's father had died a hero.

"You know that Makata has a sister, right? And that she is Seraphan?" When I nodded Adair continued. "When Takara killed Linden, Khione took her nephew for his power and went through the door Niran had created. Makata was the first of the League to cross over, and as she is one of us and thus, Zephyr is ours, we flew through to help her."

It must have been awful, your sister playing a part in the murder of the father of your child, then taking your son and travelling to another land. I didn't know Makata all too well, only that I suspected that she was the reason for the scars on James' face, and that he had once gotten close enough to injure her wings.

"The Seraphan are low in numbers. A lot of the angels that sided with Ascian were not as strong as any who had once served the League. They were quickly felled, or tried to return to the fold."

I snorted, lifting my mug to my lips. "I don't think Rieka would let them come back that easily."

"No. She did not."

I startled at the sound of Nathaniel's voice and sloshed some of my tea out of my mug. "Fucking hell, Nate. You need like a bell or something to alert people you're skulking about."

"I do not skulk." He responded; his tone clipped.

I wiggled my finger in the air. "That was totally skulking. Ugh I spilled my tea."

"Be nice to me or I won't give you the fresh cup I made for you."

Making a gimmie gesture, I took the mug as Nathaniel lowered himself into the seat, and Adair got to his feet a second after. Nathaniel inclined his head, and Adair gave me a cheery wave.

"Adair." I called after him, the angel pausing half in, half out of the door as I said. "Next time you want to gossip about men, come find me. Thanks for checking on me today. Tell your twin I'll be at training in the morning."

Adair left with a pleased look on his face as I slowly let my gaze land on the angel looking at me with a bemused expression. "Gossiping about men?"

"I'm sworn to secrecy. Now, since you chased Adair away when he was telling me stuff, you can continue on."

"Do you expect me to follow your orders?"

I let loose an exasperated sigh. "Please, Nathaniel. I would very much like to know what happened to those who sided with the Seraphan and then wanted to fall under Rieka's rule once more."

His gaze narrowed, the black of his eyes seemed to darken even more as he mused. "I do not know what to do when you ask something of me so nicely. It makes me suspicious that you are about to hurl a weapon of some sort at me."

With a shrug, I let my eyes fall on my axe. "That would mean putting down my mug and it's actually nice so I'll keep my axe to myself right now."

Nathaniel chortled, then ran a hand through his hair before he rested his hands on his stomach. "We won the first war with the Seraphan due to our over-whelming numbers. Those who might have a semblance of power my mother could use, were allowed to live, marked for the rest of eternity with the symbol of their fall from grace. The burn mark was a reminder that we had come crawling back to her, asking for forgiveness. A stark reminder if we ever dared to stand against her."

I watched as Nathaniel lowered his eyelids, the thick and long lashes caressing his high cheekbones. "The ones who the Imperium deemed unnecessary in this new world were executed and put on display."

"To deter descent."

"Yes. And to assert her power over us all. It was a deliberate action to mark me, just as it was a deliberate one to use my own power to mark those who had rebelled. My mother wanted to prove how ruthless she was, and that even her son was not exempt from punishment. Although, any who were surprised by her calculating nature were fucking fools and had forgotten how easily she killed the man she professed to love. How little she mourned him after his death."

I heard the bitterness in his tone, and while I understood it, I would never not be surprised by the depths that Rieka would go to cement her seat of power. I also found it hard to believe that she had ever loved Nathaniel's father, because I didn't think the Imperium was capable of love. But saying that would hurt Nathaniel, as much as it hurt me to think that my mother wasn't able to love me like she should because of what I was.

"Adair brought me to meet Zephyr. Scared the shit out of me when Devika pushed him over the ledge."

Nathaniel chuckled, leaning forward in his chair. "All angelic children must learn to fly when they could easily fall. Zephyr will be a strong one, his enthusiasm unwavering even when he lost his father at such an impressionable age. But then his mother has given him enough love for both of his parents."

"Why doesn't she try and keep him away from the bloodshed, then? If she could protect him from it?"

Nathaniel pondered my question, then I heard the brutal honestly in his voice as he said. "Zephyr could become something unfathomable if he was caged, unable to see his full potential. If Makata kept him from becoming who it is that he is destined to become, it could harm him. We would hope that it be centuries into his being before Zephyr has to take to the battlefield. However, should the war come for us, Zephyr has the ability to protect the weaker ones from harm, just as his father had once done. And with the right training and care, protecting the children would not result in his death."

Nathaniel searched my face, looking for disapproval and I didn't give it to him. "He's in awe of you. Apparently, the fact that you can see me when I'm invisible is awesome. I told him it made me want to punch you, and he was not pleased with me."

A slow, annoyingly sexy grin curved his lips. "Is that so? I'll make sure to make time to spend with the boy."

"I said I'd ask you and his mam if we could spar sometime. I really want to see that power of his in use. Ugh, I have power envy."

Nathaniel chuckled. "I will speak to Makata. I'm sure she would only be too happy for Zephyr to have some sparring sessions with you. And I hope that you understand that by introducing you to Zephyr, we are putting a trust in you that we do not put in most after the way in which the League became divided. I hope that it means something to you that we would."

I could tell that Nathaniel was telling me this so that I would trust him to know what was best in order to protect the people in this citadel, or more so, to protect the angels in the citadel. It made me wonder why he had not tried to ask me about the running of the barracks back home. And then I realized that Nathaniel knew I would never put my people at risk any more than he would his.

It shifted something in me then, a deeper understanding as Nathaniel rose, taking the empty mug from my hand, his fingers grazing mine. "It's good to hear that you are feeling well enough to train with Adriel. I fear he has missed your daily sessions."

That was all he said as he made to leave, his wings shifting as he strode to the door.

"Nate?" He turned back to me, his expression guarded. "I'd gut anyone who tried to harm Zephyr. You know that, right?"

Only a monster would harm a child.

Nathaniel's smile was slow, deliberate and it made me want to punch him as he just said. "I have no doubt of that. I see how you protect those you care for with little regard for your own safety."

The day of my birthday, just after midnight, I hauled my ass out of bed and went down to the study. Earlier in the day, after a mammoth training session, Adriel had pulled me aside and asked me to meet him in the study at midnight. For a stupid moment, I wondered if Adriel had remembered it was my birthday today and wanted to help me celebrate, but there wasn't much to celebrate.

I wondered if my mother would mark the day, or if it reminded her of my conception. It wasn't something we celebrated during my life, and I don't remember my mother ever giving me a present. The only gifts I'd ever gotten on my birthday were from my unit.

To say I wasn't in the best of humours as I grumbled and pushed open the door to the study would be an understatement.

"Surprise!"

The angels jumped out from behind the furniture

and I was so alarmed that I pulled my power around me for a second. I heard laughter and I let it go, placing my hands on my hips.

"You fucking idiots, if I'd a weapon I'd have thrown it at you!"

Verena, Devika, Asterin, the twins, and Nathaniel were all gathered in the study, big smiles on their faces. It was then that I took in the room. They had managed to get some happy birthday banners, had enough food to feed an army, and if I wasn't mistaken, someone had made a cake. Like a real birthday cake...I'd never seen one before.

How the hell had they managed all of this AND found out the exact date of my birthday?

"How did you know?"

Nathaniel smiled at me, amusement in his eyes. "I have my sources."

Tiernan...he'd bloody asked Tiernan.

Not that I could call him out on it without revealing Tiernan's and his little alliance and from the smug look on his face, Nathaniel knew it. I shot him a glare, but then was swept away by Verena who wanted to show me the cake. The next couple of hours was spent laughing and eating and for a time, I forget that I was still a prisoner, and let myself be happy.

Adriel came over to me, and handed me a neatly wrapped parcel.

"For me?" I asked, taking the present from him.

"Yes."

That was all Adriel said as I ripped off the paper and

held up a thin black long-sleeved jacket. I lifted my gaze to Adriel and quirked a brow. "Is this your way of saying I have terrible taste in clothes because I don't have a say in that."

Adriel chuckled, taking the jacket from me and pulled down the zipper. "No. It's for when you flirt with death again. The jacket is made with a material that is not only temperature regulated, but has some sort of material called Kevlar? The human at the market stall said that police officers used to have vests made out of it to prevent getting stabbed."

It was actually a really thoughtful gift. Adriel was trying to make sure that the next time I found myself in trouble, which knowing my record, would be sooner rather than later, I had extra protection. Guilt crashed into me and I wanted nothing more than to tell Adriel that Raisel hadn't betrayed him, that she had just protected Adair, that she had done as Nathaniel asked her to do. I stepped forward and wrapped my arms around his neck.

"Thank you. Even if you've basically called me a human trouble magnet who is only a step away from danger."

Adriel arched his brow. "And is that an unfair assessment?"

"No, but still..."

We laughed then, as Adriel held out the jacket for me to wear, telling me that he wanted to make sure it fit. And it did, like a second skin. Adriel reached out and pulled up the zip. I frowned at him, the heat of the jacket making me feel warm and a little stuffy.

When I made to take it off, Adriel gently put his hand over mine. "Don't. It's cold outside."

He walked away from me then and I felt Nathaniel's presence like an inferno behind me. His hand touched my arm. "Walk with me."

Nathaniel strode toward the door, and I followed after him, ignoring the suggestive looks from the other angels and when V smirked at me, I flashed her my middle finger, her laughter following me out. Nathaniel had already headed down toward the courtyard.

"If you are planning on killing me, best not bring me where the weapons are." I called after him, the slight twitch of his wings the only hint that I had amused him.

The moment I stepped out into the courtyard, I was happy to have the jacket Adriel had given me on because it was cold. I shivered slightly and rubbed my arms. "So what has you dragging me out here and away from the nice warm room and the really delicious cake?"

Nathaniel turned to me, a very stern expression on his face. "I wanted to give you my gift."

"If it's the pants to go with this jacket, then I approve."

Nathaniel strode over to where I stood, his hands falling to my hips and I shivered under the heat of his touch. He arched a brow, his lips curving into a sort of lopsided smirk.

"It's the cold. Don't get ahead of yourself."

"The cold. Right." He replied, tightening his grip on

my hips. Nathaniel just stood there, his hands holding me, his eyes looking at me like he was trying to look inside my damn soul. My skin felt hot, tingly, and far too tight.

"My gift?" I croaked out, feeling brave and stupid at the same time as I reached out and rested my palms on his chest. Now it was Nathaniel's turn to shiver.

"Right, your gift. I almost forgot about your gift."

I rolled my eyes at his teasing tone, and patted his chest. "C'mon, Nate. Gimmie my gift."

Nathaniel slowly lifted his gaze to the sky and I looked up and frowned. "What am I supposed to be looking for? You might be an angel, Nate, but you can't gift me the sky."

"But I can."

The only one way that Nathaniel could give me the sky was to fly me to it...

My eyes snapped down to his. "No."

"Yes. But there are a few stipulations." Nathaniel said with a grin.

My heart was beating so fast that I was wondering if I was about to have a heart attack. Adriel must have told him my wish, and since Adriel had said that he couldn't take me flying, but Nathaniel could. He knew I'd never ask Nathaniel so Adriel had asked him.

"Like what?" I asked, bouncing up and down like a hyper child.

"First, though it goes against everything ingrained in you, you must do everything I tell you." Nathaniel paused, like he expected me to argue with him but I was too excited. When he realized, I wasn't going to, he smiled and it made his harsh beauty even more striking.

"You and I will have to get really close. If that's too much, after everything that has happened to you, then I won't put your safety in jeopardy. Are you okay with that?"

I nodded eagerly. "I get it. You are the one behind the wheel and I am the passenger who must obey. Got it. One night only you have my complete and utter surrender."

Nathaniel's full lips curved into a seductive smile and my stomach flipped.

"I think I like the idea of having your complete and utter surrender, Raven Cassidy."

I slapped his chest as his arm wrapped around my waist, and he yanked my body flush against his. "Don't get used to it, bird boy. My desire to fly outweighs my need to rebel against any order you give me."

"Then let us not waste another moment. Hang on to me."

That was the only warning I got. My stomach dropped as we surged upwards at a speed that stole the air from my lungs. Nathaniel's wings beat downward, and I felt the way his body rippled as he moved them, and it felt like I was weightless.

Bursting through the clouds, I instinctively wrapped my legs around Nathaniel's waist, locked my arms around his neck. A wave if nausea rolled over me and I slammed my eyes shut, my ears popping as a gasp escaped my lips. Nathaniel slowed our ascent, his wings beating against the harsh wind. I heard Nathaniel chuckle, as my heart ricocheted in my chest and I dug my nails into the flesh at his neck.

"Open your eyes, Raven. I would never let you fall."

There was something more in his words and perhaps, had I not been scared shitless at the same time as being utterly thrilled, I might have snorted or rolled my eyes at him. Instead, I tightened my grip, felt Nathaniel suck in air, then his breath was warm against my skin as he whispered. "This is the closest you will get to flying. Open your eyes, Raven."

There was another order in his tone, but this time, I complied like I had promised, prying open my eyes and then it was my turn to suck in a gulp of air. Nathaniel had us suspended mid air, clouds all around us, so much so I could reach out and graze my fingers over them. I was surprised at how much brighter it was, despite the shadow barrier of Ascian's. Nathaniel's arm around my waist was all that kept me from plummeting from the sky if I dared to let go.

I glanced down at Ireland and wondered if this was what it was like for my mother or people who had flown to far off destinations before the world had gone to hell. Did they peer out of those metal planes and consider that this was the closest they would ever get to flying?

And yet, here I was in the arms of an immortal angel, floating above the world.

Even if it meant betraying myself, betraying all that I had ever known for the dream I had ever since I first saw an angel in flight. I knew that I couldn't pass up on the opportunity to know what it was like to have wings.

I lifted my gaze to Nathaniel's, his eyes of thunderstorms filled with so much emotion that I didn't want to try and decipher.

"Take me higher." I heard the pleading in my tone, felt Nathaniel grip me tighter before he grinned, then told me to hold on as tightly as I could. My shoulders ached, a sharp burn that spread from my shoulders and down my spine.

Nathaniel angled his body so that we were hovering and he flapped his wings and we shot across the sky. A squeal of glee tumbled from my lips as I forced my eyes to stay open, soaking in the rush of adrenaline coursing through my body. The ache in my shoulders intensified and I cried out, tears leaking from my eyes as Nathaniel stopped mid-flight, asking me if I was okay.

I nodded, unable to formulate the words to describe to him that I was mourning the fact I would never know what it was like to carry the weight of wings on my shoulders, to be able to soar through the air and feel completely and utterly powerful. It was the one thing that would have made having angelic blood more bearable, even if it meant that I would never fit in anywhere, even pretending to be human. Nathaniel could never know what I was, and no matter how much I considered that our attraction was maybe more than I cared to admit, he would sooner kill me than this constant ache of wanting to kiss me. If he knew I was an abomination,

Nathaniel would be my executioner, even though a tiny part of me hoped he wouldn't care.

"Do you want to go back?" Nathaniel asked me quietly against the rush of wind, and I shook my head.

"Not just yet. Can we just fly a little longer? Please."

A rugged smile broke out on Nathaniel's lips, as he swept his wings out and down, flying us at a steady pace, higher still until I began to shiver, my teeth chattering against the chill that still managed to seep into my bones. I was disappointed when Nathaniel began our descent back to the real world.

My legs were like jelly as we landed in the courtyard, as I detangled myself from around Nathaniel's waist, went to step back, but his arm stayed latched around me as the feeling began to come back in my body.

"That was..." I tried to convey just how much our impromptu flight had meant to me, and failed. I couldn't...it was the most wonderful gift Nathaniel could have given me. It was a birthday that I would never forget. I went up on my toes and pressed my lips to Nathaniel's cheek, the ruggedness of his stubble coarse against my lips, and I became acutely aware that his arm was still locked around my waist.

Pulling back, I lifted my gaze to Nathaniel's and I had a single heartbeat to prepare as Nathaniel let out a frustrated growl and his lips crashed into mine. His kiss kindled a flame that had lain dormant inside me until him. His teeth bit down on my bottom lip and I gasped, allowing him to thrust his tongue inside my mouth. The groan that rumbled from his chest and throat was enough to make me quiver.

Nathaniel walked forward, until my back hit the wall and still, he didn't stop devouring my mouth like he was afraid that if we stopped, even for a second, I would call a halt to this eruption. I pulled my power around us, feeling brave and daring as I yanked his tee from out of his combats and trailed my hands up his muscular frame.

Nathaniel broke the kiss to let me breath, his soft but firm lips trailing along my jaw, then my throat until I was dizzy and panting. I had thought my skin felt tight when he was holding my hips, but this felt like I wanted out of my skin. His teeth grazed the curve of my neck, sinking into my flesh, and I moaned, letting my head fall back so that he could do it again.

Panting as well, Nathaniel rested his forehead against mine, his hands running up and down my spine. I knew he was giving me time to back down, probably thought I was high from the flight. That the adrenaline rush was fuelling the fire inside me. But I knew that I would regret not being with him if I called a halt to it now.

As much as I wanted to deny it, I craved his touch.

"Raven..."

I backed off and he took a hesitant step back, and I watched the flash of uncertainty in his eyes. I did that. I made him unsure. This angel who commanded others with an authority that pissed me off, let me have this power over him. This cocky, pain in the ass angel was uncertain of me.

"I don't think I can keep up the camouflage if you keep kissing me like that. I can't concentrate enough to hold it and that's not going to change once you start touching me in more interesting places. Besides, I'm not getting naked where anyone can see."

Nathaniel looked like he didn't know how to respond, but one quick scan of his body told me exactly where his mind was. He wanted me as much as I wanted him. And yet, Nathaniel stood there, his nostrils flaring as I sauntered over to the double doors, then glanced over my shoulder and grinned, cocking a brow. "You coming?"

The look on Nathaniel's face could only be described as hungry.

Making our way down the corridor with Nathaniel right behind me, the heat of his body keeping the flames of desire still lit inside me. His hand was pressed to the small of my back as we walked up the steps. Before I got to the top step, I turned round and grabbed hold of Nathaniel's tee and pulled him in for another kiss.

There was no finesse in this kiss, it was all tongue and lips, and teeth. Nathaniel liked a nip to his lips I learned from the way his hips jerked forward when I did just that. He thrust his hands into my hair even as he plunged his tongue back into my mouth and I felt like I was having a sensory overload.

I was seconds away from tearing at his clothes when I heard a throat clear behind us, and I stumbled back, would have fallen on my ass if Nathaniel hadn't reached out to steady me.

"When you are done making a fool of yourself with the human, Nathaniel, I need a word."

Heat flushed my cheeks as I turned round to see Rieka lingering just outside my bedroom. The Imperium was dressed in a skin-tight catsuit that was moulded to her curves. Her yellow eyes skirted over me to her son, and just thinking that poured cold water over me.

What the actual fuck had I been thinking?

Nathaniel must have felt it too, because his hand on my arm held on when I tried to pull away. "Don't."

That was all he said, and I sighed, ignoring Rieka as I faced Nathaniel, leaned up to press a kiss to Nathaniel's cheek. "Thank you for my gift. I will never forget it."

Walking away from Nathaniel was harder than I imagined, as Rieka stepped in front of my door, barring my way. Her smile was triumphant. Just like with Noelle, she had won tonight and she wanted me to know it.

"Move Rieka, or I will make you."

"I just wanted to wish you a happy birthday, since I was not invited to your little party."

I didn't retort, instead I bit down hard on the inside of my mouth so that this wonderful night did not end in violence. I could have happily made her bleed, and have her injure me, but that would ruin the fact that I had flown, that the reality was so much better than this fantasy I used to have in my head.

"Mother." Nathaniel said in a tight tone. "You wanted to speak to me."

"Indeed I did. Sleep well, Raven."

The moment Rieka stepped out of my way, I stormed inside and shut the door with a slam, then threw myself down on the bed before I gave in to the urge to walk back out and put Rieka's head through the goddamn wall.

My head was all over the place after what had happened last night and I didn't know which part to deal with first. Nathaniel had not come to seek me out after whatever had transpired with the Imperium, and to be honest, I was glad. Last night after taking flight, I would have given into the adrenaline in my veins from finally getting to see what it would be like to fly and taken Nathaniel to bed.

I knew it wouldn't be like the frigid cold experience that I'd had before, that the flame that was the commander of the League of Dominious would consume me, and I would let him. It would ruin me in the end, and maybe that's what I deserved.

Then there was Hayes. I hadn't seen him since the night Nathaniel had made that blunt declaration outside the kitchen and Hayes had witnessed it all. Had he gone running to whoever it was that he was passing reports to and told them that I was compromised? Had he noticed the quiver in my body when Nathaniel touched me, only to realize that I never had when he had reached for me?

This was a mess. A big fucking mess and I didn't know how to fix things.

After a training session with Adriel, one where my friend and mentor yelled at me for being to in my head to concentrate, then smacked me in the side of the head with a kendo stick, I hung around the courtyard throwing things at a target because I didn't want to be alone in my thoughts.

Adriel had asked me if there was something the matter, but I told him I was fine just tired. His gaze had narrowed, asking me if he had done the wrong thing by asking Nathaniel to take me flying.

"God no," I had told him. "I'd never have asked him to because it would feel like I owed him something in return. It was...amazing...shit, that word doesn't do it justice. It was only a taste but it's damn addictive."

Adriel had smiled then, mollified and he had left me to attend a League meeting.

It was for that reason I was surprised to hear the beat of wings above me before an angel landed in the court-yard, then turned to face me. Her wings appeared black on a dreary day but when any sliver of light hit them, a shimmer of blue appeared as if my magic. Black hair framed her face, making the royal blue of her eyes stand out. Her lips were pressed into a firm line, and in her eyes, I saw a distain that she didn't bother to hide.

Cassiopeia wore a skin-tight leather look catsuit that clung to her curvy frame. Her metal arm guards and gloves were missing, but she had an array of little daggers around the belt on her waist. Folding her arms across her chest, Cassiopeia sighed as I continued to ignore her, a foot tapping a beat on the ground starting to grate on me a little.

"You and me need to have a little chat." She said eventually, and I snorted through my nose.

"Do we? Do we really?"

There was a mutual dislike between the two of us and Cassiopeia was one of those angels who I knew wouldn't seek me out to have a friendly chat. Cassiopeia might be one of Nathaniel's closest friends, but if I had to name the angels who hated me the most, she'd be right up there on the list, behind Abraxas, Saskia, and of course, Rieka.

"While watching you and Nathaniel interacting has been amusing, considering how much it bugs the fuck out of Saskia, I'm telling you here and now that it stops. You stop encouraging his stupid fascination with you."

I cocked an eyebrow. "Are you suggesting that I'm leading Nathaniel on?"

"I don't care what the reason is just that it just stops now. There are bigger things at stake than his wanting to fuck you." Cassiopeia said with a calmness that I was starting to feel enraged by.

"Not that it's any of your business, but I've been quite clear to Nathaniel that nothing will happen between us."

Cassiopeia rolled her eyes. "You two would have

been fucking last night if not interrupted by the Imperium."

Well...she wasn't exactly wrong there, was she...

Turning to face her, I made sure that I had a weapon within reaching distance as I placed my hands on my hips. "And what the hell does it have to do with you? I think you should just mind your own damn business. Or maybe get laid yourself, since you seem to spend too much time thinking about your *boss's* sex life."

I deliberately put extra emphasis on the word 'boss's', and that made Cassiopeia slowly blink before she spoke. "Verena might be Nathaniel's right hand, but I am his left. That's what it has to do with me. I'm the one who assesses any threat to him and you are the biggest fucking threat to him. You weaken him. Saskia, dimwit that she is, at least he didn't care about her in the slightest. But his feelings for you cloud his judgement."

My pulse started to race, but my body appeared relaxed as I taunted her. "You sound jealous, Cass."

The angel rolled her eyes, highly amused that I would think she might have feelings for Nathaniel herself. "Of you? Please spare me. You are not the only one who wants to see a change in leadership and Nathaniel is the best chance at not only becoming Imperium, but of dispatching Ascian. That was the main focus until he came up with the infuriating idea to drag you from the cold damp place you belonged."

It was a low blow, and it punched me right in the gut as I snarled, taking a step forward. "Fuck you. You do not speak for Nathaniel."

"When he is compromised, I do." Cassiopeia hurled back at me, taking a step forward herself so that now, we were within striking distance of one another. This could get bloody, really quickly and my body thrummed with the anticipation of it.

"He is playing his hand with his feelings for you." Cassiopeia continued. "Rieka knows that. Knows that Nathaniel is like his father. Zadkiel had a soft heart too with a fondness for strays."

"Like it's a bad thing for him to have a heart when his mother is such a heartless bitch."

Cassiopeia smirked, and I wanted to smack that look right off her damn face. And she knew it too, because she moved her fingers as if she was gathering that power of hers to make me do her bidding.

"How do you see this playing out between you and him, Raven? In what world do you think that Nathaniel, son of the Imperium, would be content to a life with a woman who can't give him what he needs?"

"What the hell are you talking about, Cassiopeia? You are talking in riddles."

"An heir, Raven. Every Imperium needs an heir, and not only that, but Nathaniel wants to be a father. He can never have that with you. We do not live in a world where humans and angels can share power. You will age, you will wither and die and if your track record goes according to plan, you'll die sooner rather than later. Mortal lives are fleeting. If I didn't think it would hurt him, I'd command you to stand still and I would slit your throat and leave you to the vultures to pick at your bones."

I showed Cassiopeia my teeth. "If you didn't have that voice of yours and had to fight me on an even keel, you would end up bloody. The only chance you have of taking me down is by using your power against me. So, either put up or shut up. If you have an issue with Nathaniel and his feelings, then go and fucking annoy him and leave me the fuck alone."

Her face flamed with fury, then a mask of calm crossed over her features. "I won't be goaded by you. It would take little from me to command you to walk right up to the room of the citadel and throw yourself off. I would take great pleasure in seeing your broken body on the courtyard below."

"Enough, Cassiopeia."

We both startled at the sound of Nathaniel's voice, and Cassiopeia had the good grace to look sheepish to have been caught out, but I just stood with my chin in the air, defiant until my last breath.

"Now we don't get to see me kick your ass, Cass. Such a goddamn shame."

Cassiopeia's composure shattered as she whirled on me and ordered me to my knees. My limbs complied, my knees hitting the ground with a force that banged my teeth together. I had a dagger in my hand before Cassiopeia saw it, but the moment she did, she told me to hold the blade to my own throat and I did, a nick to my flesh making me smirk, and I could smell my blood.

"Told you that you couldn't best me without using your power. Some soldier you are."

Cassiopeia hissed at me and raised her hand to strike me, but Nathaniel grabbed her wrist and yanked her backward. Her compulsion slithered off me and I surged to my feet, ready to launch at her, but Nathaniel glared at me with an expression that had me pausing.

"Enough the both of you!" Nathaniel's voice boomed like thunder and Cassiopeia flinched as Nathaniel snarled at her to just go and that he would deal with her later. She hesitated, her eyes sliding to mine and I flipped her off. When Cassiopeia made to disobey Nathaniel's order, his entire body seemed to glow a dangerous amber, a burst of flame appearing in his hand as he growled at Cassiopeia. "Go!"

She cast one last menacing glace at me, then hurried from the courtyard, taking to the skies in one burst, her wings snapping out and beating as she went higher and higher. Then that left me alone in the courtyard with a very pissed off Nathaniel.

The glow died down as he began to turn toward me, his gaze unwavering, a hint of that amber against the black of his eyes told me that he was furious.

"In my defence, I was just standing here when Cassiopeia arrived, minding my own business."

"I will deal with Cassiopeia later." Came his cold response.

Nathaniel didn't say anything for a minute or so, as I reached up and touched the cut on my neck, my fingers coming away with a little blood on them.

"She hurt you."

"Well, technically I hurt myself so..."

Nathaniel growled, the sound low and not at all human as he dragged his hands through his hair. "Stop. Stop with the wit, with the sarcasm, with the shrugging off every interaction that you have that could have ended in you being gravely injured or worse, your death. Just stop."

Ignoring the pain in his tone and what the hell it might mean, I braced myself for the onslaught of his anger. Not just his anger though, his fear that I would be hurt.

"His feelings for you cloud his judgement."

I hated to admit that Cassiopeia was right...how Nathaniel felt about me clouded his judgement...like it did Hayes when I finally realized the true extent of his feelings. It would make him a liability on the field of battle, and I would not have him hurt because he was too concerned with my safety.

"You don't get to tell me how to deal with my life, Nathaniel. You are not my commander. I am not your soldier."

His fists clenched and unclenched. "That is not what I am saying and you know it."

I swallowed hard, placing my hands on my hips again. "I know. So that is why I am telling you that what might have happened last night, won't ever happen again. This thing between us, whatever it is, let it go. The people we are hasn't changed overnight and we are still on opposite ends of this war. We are who we are and that means you and me, that can't happen. You are loyal to your people, and I am loyal to mine."

"I will not let you distance yourself from me with words meant to remind me of who we are. I know exactly who you are, Raven. And I still crave you."

"I know what you are."

Frost in his tone, I shifted my gaze back to Nathaniel, my shoulders slumped. "I know."

Between one breath and the next, Nathaniel stood before me, the heat of his flames almost scorching my skin, but it was the heat of his gaze that threatened to burn me from the inside out. His free hand reached out and gripped my chin with a bruising grasp so I couldn't look away.

"I want to hear you say it. I want to hear it from your own lips. What are you, Raven?"

For a moment, it seemed like the entire world fell away and it was just me and Nathaniel left, not even the weather dared to interfere as I wet my lips and told him. "I'm a Nephilim. I'm half angel."

He growled at me, the fingers on my chin tightening. "A filthy half-breed with deceit in her blood. You fooled us all, Raven. And now I will put an end to your pitiful existence. And if you needed any proof as to why we are monsters, this will surely be enough..."

"And now you look at me with nightmares in your eyes."

I shook my head to clear the reminder of my dreams away. I shrugged my shoulders, wanting to appear like I didn't care, when I knew dammit, that I cared too much. "Then maybe you should do what your mother wants and put me back in the prison cell. That might make you remember that as much as you let me walk around the citadel, as much as you bring me into the fold, I will never be a member of your League and I will never be a part of your world, Nathaniel. It's foolish to even think we could be anything other than prisoner and her jailer."

Jesus, Nathaniel flinched like I had struck him, and my heart ached because of it. However, it was a necessary evil. Nathaniel had once told me that he was sorry if he was the villain in my story, and yet, I wondered, in the end, would I be the one that was the villain in his story.

"We are more than what you are lowering us to be, Raven. I could kiss you now and you would fucking melt for me." Nathaniel growled, anger and sensuality in his tone.

He was right though...If he kissed me now, I'd goddamn melt for him.

Throwing my hands up in the air, I gave him a growl of my own. "Be reasonable, commander. Can you really picture it, you and me together?"

"You know I can." That was all he said.

"For how long? How long can you see this thing going on between us? Even if I survive this life of mine, I'll age Nathaniel. I'll die. I'm not an angel, I can't stand beside you and watch you rule while my people suffer. And if one day you do rule, every Imperium needs an heir, right?"

Nathaniel looked like I'd sucker punched him, and I took that as my cue to leave. He grabbed my arm, tight enough that it hurt just a little, but not enough that I couldn't yank my arm away.

"We are not done here."

"We are, Nate. It's done. We're done. Now, let me fucking go."

Our eyes clashed, and there was this moment when I thought he would kiss me, but he snatched his hand away from my arm and I stalked from the courtyard as I heard a crash. I didn't dare look back to see what destruction Nathaniel had caused. I knew once his temper had subsided, Nathaniel might come looking for me, so I kept on walking passed our bedrooms, with no destination in mind.

"It's about time you saw sense."

A snarl escaped my lips as Hayes fell into step beside me. "Fuck off, Hayes. I am not in the mood to deal with you today."

"Because you just dumped your boyfriend?" Hayes taunted me and I snapped, spinning round to shove him up against the wall.

"Fuck you, Hayes." He made to push off the wall and I slammed him back against it, hard enough that he sucked in a breath. "Green isn't a very nice colour on you."

"Neither is bitch but you are pulling it off right now."

Oh I wanted to hurt him, I wanted to unleash the wrath inside me and make him bleed like I felt like I was bleeding on the inside. I gave him one hard push and let him go, turning away to walk away before I said something I'd regret tomorrow. However, Hayes just had to cut the strands of my temper.

"You look at him like you've never looked at me. He touches you and you give him this look that I've never seen before. How can you let him touch you when, after all we've been through, you flinch when I look at you. You have to know that I'm in love with you, Raven."

Whirling back toward Hayes, he retreated with whatever he saw in my face. "I let him touch me because when he does, he sets my soul on fucking fire. He looks at me like he knows that I could kill him, but it might be worth it just to have me close. I don't want you to touch me like that because when you do, I feel absolutely nothing. No, that's a lie. I feel cold, and I hate myself. Nathaniel just has to look at me and I feel goddamn fireworks."

TWENTY-ONE

I slammed my mouth shut at the horrified expression on Hayes' face and a nervous laughter bubbled to the surface, tumbling from my lips. Slapping a hand over my mouth, I watched and witnessed as Hayes came to the realization that I didn't love him back like he wanted me to, and I could see the moment his heart broke. It would have been less painful if I had just carved it out with a knife.

"Hayes, I'm sorry..." My voice trailed off as his lip trembled and something dark and terrible inside me made me think: How could he think I would fall in love with such a pathetic creature?

"No, it's grand, Raven. You've made it crystal clear that I disgust you. But you were the one who crawled into my bed that night. You kissed me first. I would say that pretending to be one of the angels made you cruel, but you were always like this, right? Well with me anyways."

Yes, Hayes...you see me now and the illusion has been shattered... I'm not the kind of girl you should fall in love with...I'm not the hero in this story you've concocted in your head.

I was a monster and Hayes needed to know that in order to get over this infatuation he had with me, with this image in his mind. I was a monster and he could not handle the darkness in me.

Opening my mouth to retort, Hayes shoved off the wall. "Don't bother. We've got nothing else to say to one another. I won't rat you out to the elders, because I can't shut off my feelings like you can, but if it looks like you are going against orders, I will tell Tiernan. Then not only will you have to worry about the Imperium wanting your head, but the Rebels will too."

Hayes took off down the hall, the angry cut of his posture stalking away from me, and I let him go. Part of me wanted to scream and rage into the night, but I didn't deserve to take my anger out on anyone but myself. I had let my emotions get the better of me and Hayes had borne the brunt of it. I was a shitty person and an even shittier friend.

"You have to know that I'm in love with you, Raven."

I just stood there in the hallway, alone, and even when I had been held down in the abyss, I had never felt this empty and alone inside.

With a snarl I pivoted, heading back the way I came, the events of the last couple of hours replaying in my head. I felt exhausted and wanted to take the axe from my waist and take out my anger on a target. I was still furious as I stomped toward the courtyard, hoping Nathaniel was gone.

I was so lost in my thoughts that I didn't see the blow coming. Pain spread through my face as my hair fell into my eyes, then fingers grabbed my hair and wretched me to the side, slamming my head into the wall and knocked me out cold.

The door to my bedroom burst open and I was alert and awake as the figures all dressed in black surrounded me. I yanked the blade from under my bed and leapt at the attacker closest to me. I brought the hilt of the blade down on his head. He slumped to the ground, alive but unconscious. Hands grabbed for me, my wrist snapping at the force in which two of the men bent my hand so I would let go of my weapon.

Something was pressed in between my shoulders, then currents flooded through me, my spine locking as I slumped forward, only to be grabbed and held up. My hands and legs were bound and a black hood was placed over my eyes to prevent me from seeing anything. I could still feel the jolts of electricity in me, and it pissed me right off.

My bare feet dragged along the ground as the grip on me was so hard, I would have bruises that would take days to heal. I kept myself calm by reciting lines from my favourite songs. This was just another storm, another test for me to pass and I need to think clearly in order to do just that.

They pulled me along for what felt like hours, doors clanging and screams ripping through the barracks. I knew that a lot of it was theatre, a show to scare us so that if we were ever in a situation like this, that we would be desensitized to it.

There wasn't much in this world that shocked me anymore...I was pretty much numb to it all.

"My perfect soldier. That is what you were born to be."

It was when my mother sounded like she might actually love me, when I acted like her perfect soldier. When I fought, when I killed, when I became indispensable, that was when my mother showed me a sliver of affection. But it never lingered, for all too soon she remembered what I was, and then the look in her eyes changed.

My feet touched the ground and I was shoved forward with a harsh bark telling me to move. I did what I was told, trying to focus on the smells and sounds around me, even as I was shoved down onto a chair with a roughness that made me want to snarl.

The hood was pulled off my head and I blinked my eyes fast and hard to adjust to the dark. I knew this was a training exercise but those who trained us followed through as if we truly had been captured and were being tortured for information. When they had come to drag me out of the box I was kept in all night, their fingers had bruised my skin as they hoisted me out and down the stone steps.

Now, I lifted my gaze to try and take in what was around me. There were four captors in the room, two standing behind the other captive across from me, then two off to the side. My heart raced as they pulled the hood off the other captive and Hayes lifted his pain-filled eyes to mine.

My mother's words came back to me, telling me that if we were captured and the angels knew we cared for one another, they would use that to their advantage without flinching. We needed to be unwavering, we needed to be strong, we needed to hold the line.

My eyes glanced down to see that Hayes's feet were inside a bucket of water, his head lolling to the side until one of the captors used a generator to spark up some jump leads and then put them in the water. Hayes screamed so loudly I thought my eardrums might burst but I just looked at him blankly, even though I wanted to surge out of my seat and tackle him out of harm's way.

Our captors told me that I was the one who could make it stop. That all I had to do was to tell them who was in charge of the Rebels, just one name and the pain would be all over for Hayes.

And still I kept my mouth shut and my eyes open. I watched as they kept on shocking him until he passed out and was of no use to them as a ploy. Then and only then, did they start on me, rousing Hayes from unconsciousness so they could see if he would break.

But we both knew that if either of us broke, the entire process would start all over again and repeat until we learned how not to fall apart.

In my mind, I shoved all my feelings into a box and slammed it shut. I kept it closed until it was safe to open it up. It was one of the few attributes that pleased my mother, the knowledge that her child was one of the only younger soldiers who never once failed to pass a test.

Because my mother once told me that it was foolish for me to care for any of my friends too much, that I should wall off my heart against the pain for when they realized what I was, if they ever discovered it, then they would hurt me in ways that may fracture me open.

I might only have a little bit of monster in me but it was enough.

I came back to awareness as the wind howled around me and I shivered against the cold. My head was covered in a hood, not to dissimilar to the one from my memories. Pain splintered across my face as I lay sideways in the dirt, my hands were bound in front of me, and my legs were also bound tightly.

Listening to the sounds around me, I heard the sound of boots in the grass, even as the wind bellowed again. I wasn't sure who had sucker punched me, but I heard the unmistakeable shift of wings and I knew that my attacker was an angel.

Panic welled in my chest at the thought that Abraxas had managed to get one up on me and dragged me somewhere in order to do God knows what to me. But Abraxas' wings were damaged and he couldn't fly so unless he was subtle enough to carry me through the citadel to someone open enough to have the wind slap against me, my attacker wasn't Abraxas.

It was fucking hilarious that the knowledge was a relief, considering how many enemies I had in the citadel. I also ruled out Rieka, because when she decided to try and kill me, she would want to make a production out of it, a full theatrical performance that no one would forget.

That still left me with a very long list to go through.

I heard a feminine voice swear, instantly recognised

it, and I started to laugh my ass off as I sat up. The hood was yanked from over my head, my hair spilling around my face as I lifted my eyes upward.

"Hello Saskia."

The angel snarled at me, then glanced around her like she was waiting for someone to join us. Quickly taking in my surroundings, I noted that the walls of the citadel were just a blur in the distance, the night clear enough that I could faintly make out the harsh cut of the outer walls. That meant that Saskia had flown me toward Cork, my home, and more dangerously, the wastelands.

"You know, when I was running through the list of angels who were a threat to me, I didn't even consider it would be you. I didn't think you had the balls. I'm impressed."

Saskia backhanded me hard enough to split my lip. I flicked my tongue over the cut, tasted my own blood as Saskia glared at me. The poor bitch was so far out of her depth she was drowning faster than a boat with holes in it. Her fuse was short as hell, so winding her up was the fastest way to make her slip up.

"I knew you liked it a little rough, Sparkles, but that's just a love tap. Hit me harder if you want to turn me on. I promise to like it."

"Shut up, just shut up."

Saskia wore the expression of someone who had no clue what she was doing, like she hadn't thought her plan through at all. Her amethyst hair was pulled back into a severe ponytail that would have looked painful on anyone but Saskia. Her deep purple wings looked even darker against the backdrop of night, her eyes looking at me with the same startling shade as her wings.

The angel was aware of just how striking she was, beautiful even compared to many of her peers, and she usually used that as a weapon in itself. She displayed her body like a tease, showing a sample of what she had to offer, whether it was the tops she wore to show off her impressive cleavage, or the tight pants she wore to put emphasis on her dangerous curves. It would have been hella smart of her, to pretend to be this shallow bimbo and then zap them with her electricity power. More smart than I ever gave her credit for.

Today though, she wore a long-sleeved top in a camo green and combats to match with boots, like she thought that wearing that outfit would help her blend into her surrounding, but it wouldn't, not with wings and hair as distinctive as hers.

Her amulet of dark onyx stone rested in between the swell of her breasts as she reached up to fidget with it like it was a nervous habit. I didn't see any weapons on her person, but my axe lay in the grass by her feet and I tried to figure out if there was any way I would be fast enough to lunge for it.

Her purple gaze tracked mine, then she reached down and tucked my axe into a loop on her belt. "Nice try, Raven. But I'm not that stupid."

"Are you sure? Cause I don't think you had an endgame here, Sparkles. You are either gonna have to kill me or take me back. Now, if you want to cut my bindings and let me go, I'll walk my ass back to Cork and you and me, this never happened. You get to swerve the full fury of Nathaniel's temper when he realizes that you took what he considers his."

I hated myself for saying it like that but I needed to rattle Saskia, and from the flare in her eyes, it was working. She glanced over her shoulder again, and I used the distraction to yank my power over me and lunged for the axe at her waist as she turned to look back at me.

My shoulder hit her in the stomach and she let loose an oomph as we went down to the ground and I snatched the axe from her, raised it above my head ready to slash at the beautiful wings, angling the axe so that I would slice through the musculature and maybe, cause her so much pain that I could get away.

Unable to see me, Saskia blindly grasped for me, a lucky hand falling on my shoulder as she unleashed her power into me. My body seized and I dropped the axe, and my own power as her volts tried to melt my insides. I let loose a scream, then as she shoved me to the ground and straddled my waist, I ground out.

"If you fry me to death, Nathaniel will know it was you."

That had Saskia yanking her hand away from my skin as I panted, groaning as Saskia pressed her thighs hard against my sides, crushingly so. Purple electricity danced on her palms as she stared down at me, and I knew that if I so much as moved, she'd shock me again.

"Ugh, I hate you. I fucking hate you." Saskia hissed at

me, and she lifted her hand like she wanted to hit me again.

"Awh, that hurts me, Saskia. And here I thought that you just wanted some alone time with me. Although I'm picky about who I let into my bed and I've seen your taste. I think you'd drop your knickers for any hard cock that came your way...pardon the pun."

I was prepared for her slap this time, made a big show of my head turning to the side like she had hit me harder than she actually had. "You stupid human rodent. You are the reason why I'm out in the cold. Why Nathaniel won't take me back. Once you are out of the way, I can make him want me again, I know it. I was always meant to stand beside him when he becomes Imperium. And you fucking ruined that for me."

Saskia grabbed a fistful of hair and dragged me to my feet, and when I would have tried to kick out at her or something, she sent a small wave of her power into me and I let lose a moan, my insides feeling like jelly.

The angel yanked my head to the side, digging her nails into my scalp as she stared at me. "What does he see in you? What do they all see in you? You are not fucking special. I told Nathaniel that he should be looking at you and Adriel, that broken bastard overstepping with Nathaniel's property."

I barked out a laugh, which made Saskia snarl. "You told Nathaniel that I was hooking up with Adriel? Jesus, Saskia, you really are a dimwit. Adriel is my friend, though that might be something you know fuck all about since you haven't got a single friend of your own. Must really bug the shit out of you that your fellow League prefer to hang with this rodent."

Saskia wrapped an arm around my waist and was airborne a fraction of a second later, her furious snarl eaten up by the wind as we ascended. The only thing stopping me from plummeting to the ground was Saskia's arm because my hands ands legs were still bound. Her body was flush against mine, her wings moving with an angry beat as we hovered in the air and I stupidly glanced downward.

Below us the wastelands spread out as far as the eye could see. I heard the snick of the bindings as Saskia reached down with her free hand and cut the ones on my legs. A sly smirk curved her lips as she tilted her head. "Let's see just how durable you actually are, human. If the fall doesn't kill you, then the cannibal bastards will."

My heart began to gallop, and I know that the angel heard it because she smirked, leaned in as I kept my body ridged and motionless as she pressed her lips hard against mine, and I tasted strawberry on her lips.

"Kiss for good luck." Saskia laughed as she shocked me with enough volts to make me feel dizzy and on the cusp of blacking out. The angel slid her arm from around my waist, holding me out in the air with her hands under my arms, a smirk making her beautiful face ugly.

And then the fucking bitch dropped me.

THE STORY WILL CONTINUE IN

ANGEL'S TRAITOR

WINGS OF DECEIT

BOOK 3

SUSAN HARRIS

PLAYLIST

Angel's Rebel

- Tribal Blood - I Will Fight
- Neoni - READY FOR WAR
- The Linda Lindas - Rebel Girl
- Corvyx - Burn It All Down
- Paramore - Brick by Boring Brick
- Paramore - Now
- Rivals - Thunderstorm
- Paramore - Monster - Transformers Soundtrack Version
- Paramore - Ignorance
- Paramore - Part II
- blackbear - idfc
- Rihanna - Desperado
- Billie Eilish - all the good girls go to hell
- Mr. Phelps - Ready For It
- Bloc Party - Traps
- Two Feet - Go Fuck Yourself
- Rivals - Sad Looks Pretty on Me
- Rivals - Dead Flowers

259

- Muse - Won't Stand Down
- The Weeknd - Sacrifice
- Black Honey - I Like The Way You Die
- Sevdaliza - Darkest Hour
- Vanbur - Through the Dark
- MORGAN - Alien
- Asking Alexandria - The Black
- My Chemical Romance - I'm Not Okay (I Promise)
- Dance Gavin Dance - We Own The Night
- My Chemical Romance - Famous Last Words
- Bad Omens - Like A Villain
- Mike Shinoda - fine
- Shawn Mendes - It'll Be Okay
- Tommee Profitt - In The End - Emurse Remix
- ILLENIUM - Story Of My Life (feat. Trippie Redd)
- Falling In Reverse - ZOMBIFIED
- Siiickbrain - Destructible
- Cassyette - Behind Closed Doors
- Sam Fender - Seventeen Going Under
- Tommee Profitt - Will I Make It Out Alive - tofû Remix
- Holy Wars - BATTERY LIFE
- Joznez - Ready for War
- Tommee Profitt - Eye Of The Tiger - TOMER G & MARKO Dance Version
- Tommee Profitt - Reign - Deadcrow Remix
- Bring Me The Horizon - Moon Over the Castle - from GRAN TURISMO 7

- nothing,nowhere. - Sledgehammer
- Arkells - Strong
- Wolf Parade - You Are a Runner and I Am My Father's Son
- Fink - Pilgrim
- Dr. Dre - Gospel (with Eminem)
- sadeyes - i'm not okay
- Bring Me The Horizon - Can You Feel My Heart
- Timbaland - Apologize
- Ed Sheeran - Bad Habits (feat. Bring Me The Horizon)
- Nothing But Thieves - Life's Coming in Slow - from GRAN TURISMO 7
- Bad Omens - The Grey
- Steve Aoki - KULT (feat. Jasiah)
- Holy Wars - 21ST CENTURY BITCH
- CamelPhat - Silenced
- Jaymes Young - Infinity
- Mapei - Don't Wait
- Future Royalty - Losing My Religion
- Daphne Willis - BrickxBrick
- RoRo - Ladies
- AViVA - The Saint And The Sinner
- Asking Alexandria - New Devil (feat. Maria Brink of In This Moment)
- Call Me Karizma - Dead Body
- Dorothy - Rest In Peace
- Call Me Karizma - DELINQUENTS
- Boston Manor - Algorithm - Acoustic

- YUNGBLUD - The Funeral
- You Me At Six - Spell It Out
- Imagine Dragons - Bones
- Muse - Compliance
- Zayde Wølf - Heroes
- Ryan Oakes - BLOOD
- Rok Nardin - How Villains Are Made - Rok Nardin Remix
- Ki:Theory - The Prisoner's Song
- UNSECRET - Hanging On By A Thread
- Miss May I - Run This Town
- Dol Ikara - Stone Towers
- Masked Wolf - Fallout
- Holy Wars - SUCK IT UP
- The Smile - Pana-vision
- The Maine - Loved You A Little (with Taking Back Sunday and Charlotte Sands)
- Anavae - Sacrifice
- MOTHICA - LAST CIGARETTE (feat. Au/Ra)
- Two Feet - I Feel Like I'm Drowning
- Shinedown - Planet Zero
- Muse - Will Of The People
- Saliva - Crows
- Chase & Status - Hold Your Ground (feat. Ethan Holt)
- deadmau5 - My Heart Has Teeth (feat. Skylar Grey) - From 'Resident Evil'
- MOTHICA - SENSITIVE
- I Prevail - Self-Destruction
- Architects - deep fake

- DE'WAYNE - TAKE THIS CROWN (feat. Good Charlotte)
- Five Finger Death Punch - The End
- Nessa Barrett - madhouse
- PVRIS - ANIMAL
- grandson - Rain (from The Suicide Squad)
- Transviolet - Destroy Destroy Destroy
- Faouzia - My Heart's Grave
- Call Me Karizma - Rebels
- Godsmack - I Stand Alone
- Theory of a Deadman - Ambulance
- Rok Nardin - Shadows
- Måneskin - OWN MY MIND
- UNSECRET - Fallout
- Any Given Sin - Insidious
- You Me At Six - Breakdown
- Pierce The Veil - Death Of An Executioner
- Linkin Park - Lost
- RedHook - Off With Your Head
- Cody Frost - CHAOS
- NF - HOPE
- Jung Youth - Can't Take It from Me
- Apashe - Dies Irae feat. Black Prez
- Dotan - There Will Be a Way
- Bohnes - You've Created a Monster
- PVRIS - Monster
- Hidden Citizens - Smoke
- Nothing But Thieves - Trip Switch
- Nothing But Thieves - I Was Just a Kid
- KID BRUNSWICK - Stained

- Three Days Grace - Neurotic (feat. Lukas Rossi)
- Sam Tinnesz - Only Happy When It Rains
- HVDES - When I'm Alone
- MISSIO - I Wanna Fight And You Know It

Acknowledgments

None of this would be possible without an amazing team supporting me! Many thanks to:

Publishing House: CTP Publishing
Cover design: Gem Promotions
Interior Formating: Gem Promotions
Proof Reading: Ashley Brilinski

And as always:
Thank you to all the readers!
Whether this is your first book by me or you've been with me for years! I only get to do this because of you, and I am eternally grateful to each and every one of you who took a chance on this Irish author.

About the Author

Susan Harris is a writer from Cork, Ireland and when she's not torturing her readers with heart-wrenching plot twists or killer cliffhangers, she's probably getting some new book related ink, binging her latest TV or music obsession, or with her nose in a book.

Susan LOVES connecting with her fans!

SICARIUS SECURITY

Kiss of Death, book 1

Leap of Faith, book 2

Visions of Destiny, book 3

War of Hearts, book 4

Flames of Conflict, book 5

DEFY THE STARS

A Tale of Two Houses, book 1

Until Death Do Us Part, book 2

In Defiance of the Stars, book 3

Courting Darkness, a novella

THE SANGUINE CROWN

Chaos Theory, book 1

Butterfly Effect, book 2

Wicked Game, book 3

Burn Notice, book 4

Fight Song, book 5

A Lot Like Christmas Anthology

FIND REBEL STORIES ON KINDLE VELLA

The Rebel County Universe which will span eight different businesses, all intersecting with characters popping up when you least expect them.

THE REBEL BOOKS TRILOGY

Available Now:

Best Laid Plans (Rebel Books Book 1)

More Than Words (Rebel Books Book 2)

Take the Lead (Rebel Books Book 3)

Coming Soon:

The Rebel PR Trilogy

The Rebel Rescue Trilogy